Home Sweet Harmony

ROSEWOOD PRESS

Print ISBN: 979-8-9904728-5-3

Home Sweet Harmony

Copyright © 2025 by Megan Leavell

All rights reserved. Except for the use of brief quotations in review of this novel, no part of this book may be reproduced in any form or by any electronic or mechanical means, including information storage and retrieval systems, without written permission from the author.

This is a work of fiction. Names, characters, businesses, places, events and incidents are either the products of the author's imagination or used in a fictitious manner. Any resemblance to actual persons, living or dead, or actual events is purely coincidental.

Also by Olivia Miles

Stand Alone Titles
Find Me in Paris
The Gift of Christmas
The Starlight Sisters
A Wedding in Driftwood Cove
The Heirloom Inn
Christmas in Winter Lake

Sunrise Sisters
A Memory So Sweet
A Promise to Keep
A Wish Come True

Evening Island
Meet Me at Sunset
Summer's End
The Lake House

The Sweeter in the City Series

Sweeter in the Summer

Sweeter Than Sunshine

No Sweeter Love

One Sweet Christmas

The Blue Harbor Series

A Place for Us

Second Chance Summer

Because of You

Small Town Christmas

Return to Me

Then Comes Love

Finding Christmas

A New Beginning

Summer of Us

A Chance on Me

The Misty Point Series

One Week to the Wedding

The Winter Wedding Plan

The Oyster Bay Series

Feels Like Home

Along Came You

Maybe This Time

This Thing Called Love

Those Summer Nights

Christmas at the Cottage

Still the One

One Fine Day

Had to Be You

The Briar Creek Series

Mistletoe on Main Street

A Match Made on Main Street

Hope Springs on Main Street

Love Blooms on Main Street

Christmas Comes to Main Street

Harlequin Special Edition

'Twas the Week Before Christmas

Recipe for Romance

Home Sweet Harmony

HARMONY COVE
BOOK ONE

OLIVIA MILES

Ⓡ

One

Annie Baker stepped off the ferry from Boston Harbor and closed her eyes, breathing in the sweet, salty air that forever defined every good thing that had ever happened to her. It carried with it the memories of laughter, long walks on the beach, and lazy evenings spent lounging on the rickety porch swing, a faded patchwork quilt on her lap, surrounded by all her favorite books and people. It was the smell of the Cape.

It was the smell of home.

Her phone pinged the moment both of her feet touched land, followed by another alert, and then a third. Using her suitcase as a rather unreliable seat, she carefully perched on the edge and scrolled through her messages.

The first two were from her editor, Ed, at the Seattle newspaper where she'd worked for the last four years, one text urging her to include a little "heart" in her story and the second reminding her of what was at stake.

As if she needed to be told. She'd been waiting for an opportunity to move up from the local events column, and if anyone needed to be told to include "heart" in her story, it wasn't her. Aside from the features covering charity events, fundraisers, or special interests, the bulk of her articles covered weddings that could rival only a bona fide fairy tale. Most days, it felt like she wrote about nothing but emotions and love, and now she was ready for something more challenging, more rewarding, and, admittedly, better paying.

Still, she knew that this was just Ed's way of rooting for her from afar. He was one of the only bright spots about where she worked—and lived. Since moving to the Pacific Northwest, Annie had yet to adjust to the weather, and every June, she longed to be exactly where she was now: Cape Cod, Massachusetts, or, more specifically, Harmony Cove, where she would soon be once her sister arrived.

The last text was, of course, from Valerie: Running ten minutes late! Grab something at the Lobster Shack if you're hungry!

In other words, she would be more like twenty minutes late, but with the promise of a fresh lobster roll to tide her over, Annie could hardly complain.

She stood and hauled her tote bag over her shoulder and then dragged her suitcase along the dock, stopping at the ferry's beloved snack shop, where a line had formed and wouldn't let up until closing time. She let her gaze flit over the crowd, looking for anyone she might know, some she hoped to see and others she didn't. It wasn't quite tourist season yet, meaning that most people taking the ferry would be locals or part-timers. But the Cape was big enough and Harmony Cove was far enough that she didn't recognize anyone, and for that she supposed she should be grateful.

She'd always embraced the ability to return to her hometown in peace. To know that she didn't have to worry about avoiding it like her older sister, Caroline, did out of fear of running into her ex.

Living here was another story, though. One best reserved for another day, and not when she was about to enjoy a long-anticipated taste of the Atlantic's finest.

With her order in hand, she again perched on her suitcase, this time with a buttery, warm bun filled with chilled and creamy lobster meat in her hands.

If this wasn't a slice of heaven, she didn't know what was.

It wasn't Seattle, that was for sure. And it wasn't her position at the big-city newspaper, either. But maybe it eventually could be. And this week was her chance: to land the job that could finally satisfy her and to solidify the West Coast as her home base.

To confirm that she hadn't been wrong to leave Harmony Cove. That she was better off. That she had a new purpose. One where she wasn't reminded at every turn of what was missing.

She finished the last bite of her food just in time to see Valerie pull up in her white Jeep, the top down, her dark ponytail flying in the wind. Of the four Baker girls, Val was the closest to her in age, just eighteen months younger, but somehow, with her carefree attitude and zest for life, she seemed far below her years.

Or maybe Annie just felt aged by personal hardships her sister was yet to experience, and hopefully never would.

Annie ran to her as quickly as her luggage would permit,

and Valerie leaped out of the car and swooped her up into a long, tight hug.

"I missed you!" Annie said, pulling back to take a look at her admittedly favorite sister with her bright green eyes and a dusting of freckles over her nose and cheeks, acquired from too many days spent in the sun between afternoons at the beach and endless strolls for her dog walking business.

"Then why'd you stay away for so long?" Valerie countered, but it was clear from the smile on her face that she wasn't mad, just teasing.

Still, Annie's heart felt as heavy as her suitcase when she lifted it into the back of the car. That was the problem with trying to run away from your sorrow. Sometimes you ended up losing the things that brought you happiness, too.

Annie shook away those thoughts as she climbed into the front seat and, knowing how Valerie drove, fastened her belt and checked its tightness. She turned down the music so they could hear each other better, but the ocean breeze made that difficult as Val picked up speed.

"I visited last year," Annie reminded her sister.

Valerie kept her eyes on the road as she shook her head. "But that was for Thanksgiving, not last year but the year before. It's been a year and a half, Annie. Look around. It's spring."

And a warm spring day it was. Warm enough to drop the top on the Jeep. To see people out and about on a Friday afternoon, taking in the shops of Provincetown, where the ferry had landed, sitting outside at the many restaurants, having afternoon drinks and snacks as an excuse to enjoy the day.

Harmony Cove wasn't far now, and even though, as Valerie had pointed out, it had been a year and a half since Annie had last been back, it felt like yesterday. They headed south toward Turo, and she looked out over the seagrass and the dunes until she could spot the Highland Lighthouse, the first sign that they were almost there.

Almost home.

"I think I'll go to the paper first," Annie told Valerie. It wasn't just her favorite place in her hometown, but also the entire reason for her visit. "I want to see Dad and get settled at my old desk."

"It would be work that would bring you back to town," Valerie said with mock disapproval.

"Hey, it's not really a working visit. I'm covering the one-hundredth anniversary of the family newspaper," Annie told her sister. She hadn't been sure that Ed would go for the idea when she pitched it to him, but she knew that this was a story that she could get behind, put her heart into, as he so kindly reminded her, and hopefully use as the launching pad for the rest of her career.

The career she really wanted. The one she'd left Harmony Cove for, with her father's blessing and encouragement.

At least one of the four Baker daughters had to follow in their father's footsteps, and Annie had loved everything about the newspaper business since she was just a little girl accompanying her dad to his office on Water Street whenever time allowed. She used to keep all her favorite clippings, and there were plenty of those in the *Harmony Herald*; Mitch Baker prided himself on community-based stories that made everyone in town feel important and included.

She told herself that the local events column she now wrote wasn't much different, but writing about strangers—for strangers—was about as far as it could get from the small-town newspaper that had been in her family for generations.

"I'm surprised that a Cape Cod newspaper's anniversary would be newsworthy in Seattle," Val remarked as she took a wild turn, forcing Annie to grip the door handle.

"Are you kidding? In a digital age, it's an enormous accomplishment for a small family-owned newspaper to survive, much less thrive. It's a testament to the entire town of Harmony Cove, but most especially to Dad." Annie smiled as she looked out on the salt marshes, picturing her father sitting at his desk, counting down the minutes until she would see him again.

"I can drop your luggage off at the house if you want," Valerie offered as they neared the town line. "Mom's at the café all day."

Of course she was, and Annie was happy about that. She didn't expect a big party just because she was visiting. She didn't want anyone to act any differently because she hadn't been home in eighteen months. All she wanted was to come back and find that everything was the same as when she'd left. That it would always be here. Just as it always had been.

"If it's not out of your way," Annie said, knowing that the house was close enough to walk to from town, though it would be nice not to have to schlep her bag around all afternoon.

"Not at all," Valerie assured her. "I have to pick up a load of laundry, anyway."

Annie laughed. "Didn't you move out four years ago?"

She'd taken Annie's old apartment, which Annie could confirm indeed had a washer and dryer.

"What can I say? Mom does it better." Val gave a guilty smile and Annie only laughed harder.

It was true. Sharon Baker did everything better, from growing the sweetest tomatoes to making the creamiest clam chowder. Their house wasn't always the tidiest, but it was the most lived-in and the most loved. It was a house that had seen four girls come through it, banging the screen door over and over, scuffing the floors, scratching the walls from where their artwork was hung and treasured. That was what their mother did best. She created the happiest home.

And Annie couldn't wait to be back.

"She said she'd have a family meal one night," Annie said. "Knowing Mom, that means she'll be making all my favorite foods."

"Maybe I have to move away to get my favorite meal made," Valerie said wistfully, but it was clear that she was joking.

"You wouldn't really move away, would you?" Annie asked, not sure why the thought of it bothered her so much. Caroline had moved to Philadelphia three years ago, and their relationship had been reduced to infrequent phone calls. She hated the thought of losing touch with her other two sisters the same way.

"Move?" Valerie grinned as she shook her head. "How could I ever leave this?"

How indeed, Annie thought as they both fell silent. Harmony Cove was just in front of them now, the shingled buildings lining the road that backed up to the water, and the harbor clear in the distance, large masts peeking up above the rooftops on the horizon. And the water, as blue as her eyes, as Annie's father used to tell her.

She knew it was only April, but looking on to the bay now, she had the urge to run out to the water and jump in, the way she used to do the first warm day of summer when she was a kid.

Valerie swerved to a stop outside the gray building that had housed the *Herald* for three generations. She gave Annie a funny look while Annie fumbled with her hair, now wind-blown and knotted.

"I know, I know. I probably look like I slept on the beach," Annie said, using a line that their mother often deployed when they were younger and didn't want to get ready for school. She dug around in her handbag for a brush, but then decided it didn't matter.

Her father wouldn't care what she looked like. And her aunt Marcy—well, she cared far too much about everything that happened in this town to worry about appearances.

"So you've talked to Mom about your visit, then?" Valerie shifted in her seat, tipping her head.

Annie raked her fingers through her tangled hair, but it was useless. "Only to let her know my plans. She's so busy at the café, we don't talk much."

Valerie nodded in agreement. They both knew that the Sweet Harmony Café took up most of their mother's waking hours, not that anyone ever complained. Growing up, the girls happily divided their time between the house, the café, and, for Annie, the newspaper office.

"And Dad?" Val slanted her a glance. "He knows you're back?"

"Well, I assume Mom told him," Annie replied as if such a thing needed to be stated.

Valerie licked her lower lip. "Mom has been really busy, like you said. Maybe she hasn't told him."

Annie laughed. "That would be strange, but if so, then I guess he's in for a surprise!"

She looked up at the building, imagining her dad inside, sitting quietly at his desk, or maybe going over some notes with one of the reporters, his reading glasses resting on the tip of his nose.

"Annie—" Valerie started. But when Annie raised her eyebrows, she shook her head, stopping herself. "We'll catch up more later."

"Can't wait!" Annie leaned over and gave her sister a peck on the cheek. "We have so much to talk about!"

"That we do," Valerie said with another funny smile as Annie hopped out of the car and hurried up the steps of the *Harmony Herald*.

Annie smoothed her hair again and then set her hand on the doorknob, taking in the wooden sign that had been there since before she was born, turning only to wave goodbye to her sister, who seemed anxious about letting her go.

Was it that big of a deal to drop in on their father at work unannounced?

Maybe he already knew she was coming. Or maybe, like Valerie had said, it could be a big surprise.

And who didn't love surprises?

"*Annie*? Annie Baker?"

Annie turned at the sound of the unmistakable voice of her aunt Marcy—a woman who claimed that she wasn't easily shocked, at least in this small town, but who relished in drama all the same.

"That's my name," Annie said with a smile as she stepped forward to greet her father's younger—and only—sister.

Aunt Marcy smelled like the same lavender soap she'd used all her life, but then Aunt Marcy didn't like change, at least not in her own life. She thoroughly enjoyed all the ups and downs and twists and turns that other people experienced, and she happily wrote all about them, thinly veiled, of course, from the safety of her large wooden desk under the window that looked out on to Water Street and all its happenings.

"Well, isn't this a *surprise*!" Marcy pulled back to stare at Annie, her eyes, which were always a little magnified behind her thick glasses' lenses, widening.

So Valerie had been right. Huh. Usually, the chain of communication in the family started with their mother; if their father had known of Annie's arrival, then Marcy would have sniffed it out of him.

Was Annie's mother so busy at the café that she'd forgotten to mention Annie's visit? Annie did a quick replay of their conversation last week, which had been brief.

Perhaps her mother had thought it was intended to be a surprise, given that Annie had asked her not to mention the topic of her article.

Yes, surely that was it.

Turning her attention back to Marcy, she gave her a teasing smile. "I know how much you like surprises." Especially when she had a front-row seat.

"Well, who doesn't? Except..." Marcy blinked a few times. "This is *quite* a surprise. Either your father didn't tell me or you didn't tell him."

"More like my mother didn't tell him," Annie said with a shrug.

Marcy's large eyes blinked slowly. "No, I suppose she wouldn't have told him."

"Is he here?" Annie asked, craning her neck over her aunt's shoulder to see if her father's office door was open.

"He's here, dear," Marcy replied. "Where else would he be? But let me look at you. You get prettier every time I see you, I swear. And your hair... A new look?"

Oh, that Marcy. Nothing got past her.

"Thanks to the ocean breeze and Val's heavy foot." Annie laughed. She glanced impatiently down the hallway again. The last door on the right was closed. "So my dad's in his office?"

Marcy nodded. "He is but—"

"Shh," Annie whispered to Marcy as she hastened down the narrow hallway, her aunt hot on her heels, no doubt eager to take in Mitch Baker's reaction to the sight of his second oldest daughter, home at long last.

Marcy lived for this type of thing, and over time, the

family, and even the townspeople, had learned to indulge her.

"I don't think he's alone in there, dear," Marcy whispered when Annie reached for the doorknob.

Annie hesitated long enough only to consider whom he might be meeting with: Ray Cunningham from the weekend edition, or maybe the mayor, who liked to stop in and give Mitch the scoop about town matters—the closest thing to hard news that the *Herald* would ever cover, other than the police blotter, of course, which was Marcy's favorite column, other than her own.

"I'm sure whoever it is will be someone I'm happy to see," Annie told her aunt confidently, not in the least bit deterred when she saw the way Marcy's eyes popped and stayed that way.

With a sloppy grin on her face, Annie turned the knob, pushed open the door, and cried, "Surprise!"

Only this time, the surprise was on her. Because there, sitting across from her father's desk, in her favorite visitor's chair, the one she used to curl up in and scribble in her notebook, writing so-called stories about the silly things transpiring in her sisters' lives, was the one person who had sworn he was leaving this town—and her—behind him.

"Annie." Sean's handsome face seemed to pale as he stared at her. He had a leather portfolio open on the desk, a pen in his hand, and new creases on his face, but other than these small differences, he looked exactly the same as he had the last time she'd seen him—six years ago. His brown hair was cut a little shorter, and his shoulders were a little more filled out, but his dark eyes were just as intense as ever when they locked with hers, and the mouth that she once kissed, ever so casually, gave a hint of a smile.

One that Annie could not, and would not, match.

The room fell completely still, and Annie was all too aware of the pounding of her heart and the heat of Marcy's breath close on her neck.

"Annie!" Her father recovered first, standing quickly, his arms open as he took three long strides around the desk and pulled her into his arms. "This is a surprise."

Why hadn't Valerie warned her? Or Marcy?

Annie craned her neck to look at her aunt, whose eyes shone with glee.

But then of course Marcy hadn't told her that Sean was not only back in Harmony Cove but here, in her family's place of business, and in her father's office. It was so much more interesting to watch the fallout.

Well, Annie wasn't about to give her—or Sean for that matter—a show.

"Hey, Dad," she said, managing to keep her voice from shaking along with all of her limbs, which seemed to have gone instantaneously numb. "Sorry to spring myself on you. I guess that Mom forgot to mention that I was visiting this week."

Her father's brow pinched for a second before he smiled broadly. "And miss this moment? This is the best thing that's happened to me in, well, months."

If only she could say the same. Her smile was watery at best.

Seeing the tenderness in her father's soft blue eyes, Annie felt her heartstrings pull tight. Leave it to her dad to always make her feel a little better, even now, when the one person who had a way of making her feel completely terrible was sitting close enough to touch.

Oh, no. A sudden thought took hold, and Annie felt her entire body seize up as Sean closed his portfolio and stood.

He wouldn't hug her, would he? And what would she do if he tried?

But no, *no*, he was the one who had ended things. He was the one who had chosen a big career over this town. And her.

He clearly didn't have enough interest in her then and he certainly wouldn't have any now.

Not when... Oh, no. Annie felt her breath catch when she thought of her hair. Her knotted, tangled, windblown hair. She'd been traveling since six o'clock this morning. She had lobster breath, possibly some food stuck in her teeth. And her *hair*. Had she mentioned her hair?

She glared at Marcy. Really, the woman should have at least handed her a brush. She was family, after all.

Sean's gaze met hers and rested there for a moment, leaving Annie's heart to jackhammer against her rib cage.

"I'll leave you to your reunion," Sean said tightly, finally breaking his stare. He paused in the doorway, only because Marcy was making a stubborn point of barricading his exit, and turned to give Annie a hesitant look.

"It's good to see you again, Annie."

Annie gave a little sniff in return. She could hardly return the sentiment. And besides, even if she'd wanted to say something, her mind had gone blank and her mouth had gone dry and there was so much to say that she wouldn't even know where to begin.

Why was he back and why was he here being at the top of the list.

"Thank you, Marcy," her father said, indicating that his sister could also take her leave.

Marcy hovered for a moment and gave a little sigh of disappointment as she stepped out into the hallway, pulling the door only partially closed behind her.

Mitch reached out and closed the door firmly, raising his eyebrows at Annie in a conspiratorial way.

It brought a smile to Annie's lips and a warmth to her chest—at least, for a moment.

"What is Sean doing here?" she whispered to her father.

He sighed as he leaned against the desk. "He's back in town. It's new, and that's probably why this is the first you're hearing of it. If I'd known you were visiting, I would have told you, honey."

Annie nodded. That was fair, and she knew he would have. Her mother was another matter.

"But why is he here in your office?" Like herself, and her father, Sean was a journalist, only he'd made it clear long ago that he had no use for a small-town paper.

Her father pulled in a long breath and held it for a moment. "He works here, honey."

Annie gaped at her father. "He *works* here? Sean works *here*, at the *Harmony Herald*." There was a long beat of silence and then she released a laugh that held no amusement. Just shock. And confusion. And hurt.

"Chasing hard news was why he left," she insisted,

thinking of how determined he'd been to make a name for himself, and he'd done that, first in Washington, DC, and later, overseas as a foreign correspondent. As far as she knew, he'd never even come back to Harmony Cove for a visit and now she was supposed to believe he was living *here*?

"People change," her father said gently.

Annie stared at her father.

Nope. She wasn't buying it. Not Sean Morrison. He didn't change. Not until he changed his mind—about staying in this town. About her.

"I'm sorry for the shock, honey. We can talk about it more later, if you'd like, privately."

In other words, it was probably best if Annie left. She couldn't get out of there soon enough.

"Have you...talked to your mother lately?" Her father peered at her closely over the rim of his glasses in that journalistic way that Annie always found so endearing.

"No, and now I wish I would have. But I'll go and see her now," she said. Oh, yes, she would. The café was only a few blocks away, and even though it was probably closing any minute if it hadn't already, her mother always stuck around for a few extra hours to prep for the next day. Sharon Baker had some explaining to do. Surely, she could have mentioned this sooner, unless she thought it would keep Annie from coming home.

And it would have, Annie realized.

If she'd known that Sean was here, at her family's newspaper of all places, she wouldn't have come back. She'd have stayed in Seattle, writing about charity parties and other people's weddings instead of her own. She wouldn't have her pulse on a great, inspiring story that might earn her a long-awaited promotion.

She might not have a promotion at all.

And she still might not—if she blew this opportunity.

Her resolve tightened, she turned to the door and walked out into the hallway, past Marcy, who had been standing two feet away near the water cooler this entire time.

Sean had derailed Annie's life once before. But he wouldn't get away with it a second time.

Two

Sean stared at his computer screen, but his mind was on anything but his five-o'clock deadline. In the four months since he'd been back on the Cape, he'd managed to not think about Annie much after the first initial week. In those early days, it was all he could do not to think of her. How her head used to rest on his shoulder when he was driving out to the ocean, her long auburn hair spilling over his arm, tickling his skin. How she'd laugh until she snorted, then slap a hand over her mouth to cover her embarrassment. How they'd sit on a faded and worn picnic table on the sand, eating lobster rolls and sipping cold iced tea, watching the tide roll in until the sky turned dark, content with nothing more than the sound of the water and each other's company.

And he had been content. More than content. He'd been happy. The last time he was happy was in Harmony Cove, with Annie, and being back in town without her felt strange and wrong. It took a full week to get his footing, to not look over his shoulder or reach for the phone, to stop thinking that they could pick right back up where they'd left off six years ago.

But Annie was gone. She'd moved to Seattle a little over four years ago, for reasons he didn't understand until Mitch raved about the opportunity that had come along, and how he'd encouraged Annie to take it. Sean had kept tabs on her over the years on social media or the occasional internet search when the days got too long and the nights were too lonely, and the transfer had come as a shock to him at first. Annie was a homebody. She loved this town as much he did—not that she'd believe that—and to hear her father tell it, she visited often. Sean had been bracing himself for the holidays, telling himself that when he saw her again, he'd be ready.

But he hadn't been ready today.

Annie. His mind was fresh with the image he'd tried to banish for so long. Those bright blue eyes, that soft auburn hair, the smile that made his heart turn over—even if it wasn't for him. She looked just as good as she had the last time he saw her, when he'd told her he was taking the job in DC. When he'd broken her heart.

Sean pushed back the memory of that day and clicked on his keyboard, bringing his laptop to life. He took a sip of the coffee that had gone cold while he was talking to Mitch, but he didn't dare go into the hallway for more. Annie could still be here. In her father's office. Worse, on her way to see him.

And what would he say? How would he explain himself, when he'd so brutally cut things off six years ago, telling himself that it was the only way? Convincing himself, or trying to at least, that it was best. That it made it easier for him to leave. To never look back.

He scanned the article he'd been working on, even though it was only half-finished. He knew that this piece on the controversial new bayfront hotel development wouldn't take him more than another thirty minutes to draft, but he felt stuck and distracted. And right now, he wanted to be anywhere but at this desk, and not because it was at the *Harmony Herald*, the newspaper he'd traded for a national publication, even though bigger wasn't always better.

Mitch had been good to offer him a second chance. But then, the Bakers were good people.

Especially Annie.

A knock at the door made him almost spill his coffee, and before he could prepare himself for the possibility of it being Annie, the doorknob turned and Marcy's head poked inside, a giant grin spread across her face.

Sean stifled a groan as the woman let herself into his personal space, holding her favorite mug in the shape of a gray cat, the curved tail being its handle.

To the best of Sean's understanding, Marcy was severely allergic to cats and therefore didn't own one, but longed to nonetheless.

"Hello, Aunt Marcy," Sean said, and then silently cursed himself. It was an old habit. Seven years of dating one of the Bakers had made them all feel like family once, and being back here made him almost feel like one of the clan again.

That was until Annie had shown up and reminded him otherwise.

If Marcy noticed the slip, she didn't correct him. "Annie just left," Marcy told him.

"Oh." Sean felt the wind come out of him, and he didn't bother to hide his disappointment even though, from the way that Marcy was studying him, he knew that he should.

Annie had left without coming to speak to him. She had come and gone without saying anything after all this time.

Was this how it was going to be, then? The silence would continue even now when they were both here in Harmony Cove?

"I'm just checking in to see how you're doing," Marcy whispered as if they were in cahoots on some big secret. "You know, with Annie being back and all."

"Fine," Sean said automatically because it was a phrase he'd gotten used to repeating, even though he wasn't the least bit fine. Not about the reasons for him being back in town. Certainly not about her leaving without another word. Not about seeing Annie.

But the truth was that he hadn't been fine in a long time, not since he'd packed his bags and boarded that ferry, and never returned to the Cape. Until now.

Marcy stared at him from behind her thick glasses, as if waiting for him to crack, break down, or maybe burst into tears.

As much as he was sure a part of her would love to see him do any of those things, Sean forced a grin.

"Must be nice for Mitch to have his daughter home," he said. Then, because he couldn't resist, as casually as he could muster and struggling to meet Marcy's eyes, he asked, "Is she...staying for long?"

"Is that the reporter asking the question or the ex-boyfriend?" Marcy asked primly.

"Both." Sean raised his hands. Guilty as charged.

Marcy laughed and seemed to relax a bit, the old familial connection once again taking precedence. "Hon, I know about as much as you do, and that's not much."

"Why, Marcy, I'm disappointed in you!" Sean grinned to show that he was kidding. Since coming to work for the paper, he and Marcy had developed an easy rapport, and he knew that the older woman enjoyed his teasing.

Just so long as she didn't misinterpret it as flirting, he thought to himself. It was legend that Marcy had been on the prowl for a husband for years, and the older she became, the wider her criteria spread. Last week, one of his buddies from high school told him over drinks that he could have sworn Marcy rubbed his backside when he scooted past her to get to his barstool. Marcy was known to frequent all the hot spots on weekends; she claimed loose lips gave the best scoop.

"Isn't it your job to know everything that's going on in this town before anyone else?" he asked.

"Technically, yes," Marcy said without a shred of irony. "And you know that my Harmony Happenings column is the most popular column in our newspaper."

No doubt. Sean grinned wider.

"But it seems that when it comes to family matters, I'm out of the loop. And maybe I'm not the only one." She gave him a knowing look.

The suggestion of what Marcy was implying filled Sean's gut with unease. He thought of Annie when she first burst into her father's office. Those blue eyes, as deep as the ocean. That smile, as big and wide as the Atlantic itself.

"Does she know about her parents yet?" Sean asked carefully. He couldn't help it; even now, he still cared. About Annie. About her family.

About this town.

"I'm not sure," Marcy said with a frown. "But I happened to hear her say that she was on her way over to the café."

Sean lifted an eyebrow. "You *happened* to hear?" But he was smiling now because Marcy was harmless. Nosey, but still, harmless.

"Looks like she's in for another surprise," Marcy said knowingly as she moved away from the doorjamb and slipped back into the hallway.

Yep, Sean thought as he went back to staring at his computer screen. And a nasty one.

Like the newspaper, the Sweet Harmony Café had been in the family for generations, and, like the newspaper, it was Annie's second home, the place where she'd grab a snack after school or help out in the kitchen, even though her youngest sister, Molly, had always been much more interested in that task. It was the place where Annie always knew she'd run into a familiar face, happy to greet her, and where her mother could always be found making the rounds and chatting with the locals.

Even though Annie had just eaten, her mouth watered at

the smell of her mother's recipes when she entered the cozy room with creamy white walls and rustic floorboards. There were no white tablecloths here, just a bunch of dark wood tables and cross-back chairs, most of which were filled now, even though it was midafternoon, and the lunch rush was over.

Molly was the first to spot her, and she scurried around the counter, pulling Annie into a hug before Annie could even say hello.

"Mom told me you were coming in today but I didn't know when! I've been watching that door all day long." Molly's smile lit up her eyes, the same shade of green as Valerie's and their mother's.

Her baby sister's excitement made Annie force all thoughts of Sean from her mind, even though that was easier said than done. He'd looked good. Too good. She'd secretly hoped that the years had been hard on him, that if she ever saw him again he'd be worse for the wear, not every bit as appealing as he was the last—and final—time they'd kissed. Her stomach was still fluttering from the brief interaction and her knees were wobbly as she moved to let a customer get by her.

Well, she wouldn't let him taint this visit for her. She'd just write her article from her parents' house instead of the newspaper office. It would be less distracting, anyway, what with Marcy and all.

"Glad to know that Mom told someone about my visit," Annie said. "She forgot to tell Dad."

Molly's smile slipped, and she turned to look back at the kitchen door. "About that—"

"Is Mom here?" Annie asked, following her sister's gaze. She could picture her mother right now, her gray-blond hair pulled back in her usual low bun, her favorite apron bearing a faded logo of the café tied at her waist, her eyes bright with energy, and a tired but satisfied smile gracing her mouth.

They were hard workers, the Bakers, but they all loved what they did.

Well, maybe not Annie. Not these days, at least. But she was doing something about that. This was her week to turn things around, to get back on track after Sean derailed their plan.

He certainly wouldn't be doing that again.

"She's in the kitchen." Molly bit her lower lip. "She's been…very busy lately."

"Too busy to tell me about Sean being back in town?" Annie stared at her sister.

Molly's cheeks flushed with guilt. If there was one family member capable of shame, it was this one. She was a sensitive, gentle soul, like their father. "I wanted to tell you when he first moved back but Mom was afraid that if you knew, you'd never visit again."

As suspected. "I figured that was the case. And maybe she was right. But I'm here now, and I've seen him, so that's over and behind me."

Molly's eyes widened. "You saw him? Where?"

"At the newspaper," Annie replied. The memory of walking into her father's office and seeing the only man she'd ever loved filled her with a wave of emotions that started in her stomach, swooped straight up to her heart, and then dropped back down to her stomach. Even after all these years, those deep-set eyes affected her, only this time, she wished they didn't. She forced her attention on her sister and shrugged. "We said hello. Or he did. Come to think of it, I don't think I said anything to him at all."

Molly's shoulders dropped for a moment. "That's so sad. You two were so in love once!"

Annie almost laughed. "What were you expecting, Molly?"

"I don't know," Molly said. "I guess I just thought with him being back in town..."

Annie stared at her sister in disbelief. Did she not remember what the man had done to her, announcing he was leaving Harmony Cove for good just when she thought their life together was about to officially begin?

"You're still reading those romance novels, aren't you?" Annie shook her head. Their cousin, Emily, was kind enough to offer a family discount at her bookshop, which Molly all too happily supported.

Annie felt her eyes hood. Molly was showing their age difference, even though that wasn't much of an excuse. By twenty-seven, Annie had already fled to Seattle, where she didn't know a soul, while Molly was still living at home, or technically in the guesthouse over the garage, working for the family business.

It sounded nice. It sounded like the way things might have been.

A fresh wave of anger formed a hard knot in Annie's stomach.

"The guy broke up with me to build his career, Molly. He thought he was too good for the *Herald*, too good for this town, and too good for me." Her voice rose with emotion, and she dropped it to a near whisper when she added, "He didn't even ask me to go with him."

"But would you have wanted to go?" Molly said gently. The old soul poked through. It was always there; even when they were little girls.

Annie didn't need to consider the question. She wouldn't have wanted to go, because there was a time when she didn't think anything could ever drive her from this town or her plan to work at the family paper, and she supposed that Sean knew it, and maybe that was why he hadn't asked, but it sure hadn't stopped him from leaving.

The kitchen door swung open, and her mother's voice called, "Is that Annie I hear all the way in the kitchen?"

Annie turned from Molly, feeling immediately relieved at the mere thought of seeing her mother's comforting face again, but when she saw the woman walking toward her, she froze.

"*Mom?*" Her mouth felt dry, and she couldn't help but stare.

"What do you think?" Her mother's eyes shone, probably mostly due to the purple eyeshadow that covered her eyelids. She bit her lip—covered in shimmery hot pink lipstick—coyishly, and cupped the bottom of her new bob haircut, complete with pink highlights.

Everything about her was pink—other than the eyeshadow. Gone was the usual white T-shirt and well-loved jeans. Instead, under her apron, she wore a bright pink boat-neck sweater and matching capri pants.

Even her shoes were pink.

And her nails, Annie thought with alarm as her mother stepped forward to hug her.

Annie could barely bring herself to pat her mother's back. She felt like she was hugging a stranger. But it felt like her mother. And it smelled like her mother (ah, the chowder!).

Still, Annie pulled away quickly, continuing to stare at this strange creature before her. "Mom, I..."

"What do you think?" her mother asked again, more impatiently this time.

"I think you're very...pink." Annie heard Molly snort and then smother a laugh behind her.

Her mother, however, seemed thrilled by the observation. "It's my new color. Well, other than the eyes, because they say that shades of purple accentuate green eyes."

As did three coats of mascara, it would seem.

Annie was silenced by her confusion. Since when did her mother wear makeup at all? She was a natural beauty—everyone on the Cape said so—a woman who had aged with grace and elegance, who looked at least ten years younger even though she spent more than her fair share of time in the sun every chance she had, mostly tending to her vegetable garden, or taking long walks on the beach. A woman whose beauty regimen consisted of a bar of soap and a thick moisturizer.

"Why?" Annie asked. Then, after clearing her throat, she said, "I mean... Why pink?"

Surely her mother was too old for a midlife crisis, but this had all the hallmarks of one.

"Pink is known to bring out the natural color in a

woman's face. To give her a...youthful glow." Sharon smiled proudly, and Annie just continued to stare. There was nothing natural about this new look. "Besides, it was time to mix things up."

Her mother tossed a dishtowel over her shoulder with a defensive huff.

Mix things up? But Annie liked things just the way they were. She glanced at Molly, who seemed frozen in her spot. In other words, no help.

"Are you changing the café, too?" Annie asked with growing alarm. She loved this café just the way it was. Everyone in town did. It wasn't just the place to go for a warm bowl of soup or a familiar face, it was where friends and family gathered year-round, always knowing that they'd be welcome, all because of this woman. Annie's mother.

"Oh, no. Nothing crazy like that!" Sharon tutted.

Right, because changing the menu would be crazy, not, say, coloring one's hair pink and buying out the nearest makeup counter.

"When did this all happen?" Annie asked, shooting Molly a hard look as she edged back around the counter, again wondering why everyone in her family had failed to keep her up to date. Was she really so removed from their lives being in Seattle?

But even as she thought it, she knew that it was true. As Val had pointed out, her visits were less and less frequent, and for shorter amounts of time. She'd used work as the excuse, but it wasn't true.

Coming back here only ever made returning to Seattle that much harder. It filled her with longing for the comfort of the lazy evenings she'd spend with her sisters and cousins, for the big family weekend meals, for afternoons in this very café, and mornings at the busy *Herald* offices. For the salty air and the familiar smells and sights and people she'd known all her life.

It reminded her that she had nothing worth returning to Seattle for, and so much to leave behind here, and that saying as much would mean admitting failure.

And the Bakers didn't fail. They didn't get knocked down, either.

Her father had pulled strings to get her that job, hoping to get her out of her lingering rut after Sean moved away. He'd encouraged her, cheered her on every step of the way, and basked in her success from afar, and in return, she'd vowed to make him proud. This week, she'd do just that.

Annie stared at her mother, or the woman who had taken over her mother's body and decided to "mix things up," and said with a forced smile, "What brought on this new look, Mom?"

Sharon gave Molly a little nod and said, "Can you check on my rosemary loaves, hon? Don't want them getting dry."

"Sure thing, Mom," Molly said eagerly. "And I'll cover the counter, too. Don't worry about a thing." With that, she wasted no time slipping through the kitchen door.

Sharon motioned to the nearest open table and said to Annie, "Sit. I'll bring you some chowder."

Even the thought of a warm bowl of creamy clam chowder no longer sounded enticing. "I'm fine, Mom," Annie said, though she was the furthest thing from it. "Just... sit. Talk. Tell me what's up."

No wonder her father had looked so stressed when she told him she was heading this way. Even an accomplished journalist would struggle to put this transformation into words, let alone explain it.

They took their seats, and Sharon spread her hands out on the table, all ten glossy pink fingernails on full display. Wait. Were those press-on nails? But her mother never got manicures, not even when the four sisters treated themselves and asked her to join them. She always claimed she couldn't get her hands into the dirt and tend to her garden if she was worried about messing up the polish.

Annie glanced at the counter, where Molly had now resumed her station, watching carefully from a dozen feet away. Surely there must be an explanation. Surely there must be a reason for this sudden change.

Her mother opened her mouth, closed it, and then blinked a few times. "If you must know, your father and I are no longer together."

Annie heard Molly's footsteps practically sprinting back to the kitchen door.

She stared at her mother; all other cheerful conversation from surrounding tables seemed to go deathly quiet. Her heart was pounding so hard that she could hear it in her ears. "What do you mean, *no longer together*?"

But as she asked the question, a small part of her became all too aware of exactly what her mother meant, while the other part, the bigger part, couldn't accept that. It was preposterous. Unthinkable!

Her breath was shaky as she stared at her mother, waiting for an answer as much as she feared it.

"I mean that we're not together," Sharon said with a huff.

Annie could only blink at her mother, who was now folding her arms across her chest.

"You've been married for..." Annie stopped to do the math. Caroline was two and a half years older than her, and she was born on their parents' third anniversary—a happy surprise, as they liked to say.

After today, Annie was starting to wonder if there was any such thing as a happy surprise.

"Thirty-five years," Sharon replied with a sniff. She spread her hands out on the table and studied her obscenely long and, admittedly, perfect nails for a moment. "And on my thirty-fifth wedding anniversary, I woke up and decided that I was done."

"Done?" Annie stared at her mother in bewilderment. Images of her parents dancing in the kitchen when their favorite song came on the radio swam to the surface, blurring her vision as hot tears threatened to fall. She could still hear her mother's laughter when her father would lean over and whisper some secret joke, just between the two of them. She could see his grin when she walked into the house after a morning out in her garden, her hair flecked with dried leaves, her cheeks flushed.

"Done." Sharon gave a firm nod. "Like a cake."

Annie gaped and then, after a moment, firmly closed her mouth.

"But you love Dad," Annie pressed, blinking away the tears before they could fall. "And he loves you."

Sharon snorted. A family trait, and one that Annie had inherited, one of so many.

"If that's the case, then he has a funny way of showing it!"

Annie looked toward the counter for any sign of her sister, but it seemed that Molly was determined to stay hidden in the kitchen. Annie desperately wished that she could join her.

Instead, she sighed heavily and gave her mother a long, hard look.

"Did you guys have an argument?" Her parents never argued, at least not in front of their daughters.

Sharon looked tired. "Look, I know this is difficult to accept, Annie, but your father has accepted it. He's moved out."

"Moved out?" Annie cried. Then, realizing that she'd caught the attention of the neighboring table, she lowered her voice to a whisper. "To where?"

Her mother shrugged. "Beats me. Though, I might have heard something about him living above the newspaper offices." She scratched her neck and stared out the window.

A tell, Annie suspected, not that her mother was prone to lie. But then her mother wasn't prone to wear hot pink lipstick or say, leave her husband, either.

"Wait," Annie said as she reviewed the facts thus far. "You said that you decided all this on your wedding anniversary."

"That's right," Sharon replied, shifting her gaze back to her.

Annie struggled to look her mother in the face, or what she could see of her face, behind all that makeup.

"But that was in September! Are you telling me that you've been separated for more than six *months*?"

"Has it already been that long?" Her mother looked momentarily stunned but then gave her shoulders a little wiggle as she fluffed her hair. "I guess the saying is true. Time flies when you're having fun!"

Only, *was* she having fun? Annie wasn't so sure, and she didn't think it was denial on her part. Despite the glittering makeup, her mother's eyes didn't shine like they used to after a morning in her garden or a long day at the café.

"Mom." Annie heard her voice break and knew that her mother had, too.

Sharon's gaze softened as she reached across the table and took Annie's hands into hers. They were calloused and familiar, and Annie felt herself relax for the first time since she got out of Valerie's car—until one of the fake nails stabbed her in the palm.

"I wanted to wait and tell you in person. Your father agreed. Please don't be mad at us. This has nothing to do with you girls. This is between your father and me."

"But you're my parents," Annie whispered, fighting back tears. "We're all one family. It won't be the same if you and Dad aren't together anymore. What happened, Mom?"

Any emotions that her mother might have had regarding this separation seemed to have worn off months ago. She said matter-of-factly, "Nothing happened. No one had an affair, at least, not a real one. Your father's first love has always been that newspaper, and you know that."

Yes, Annie did, but that was his career. It couldn't be compared to loving another person. And wasn't that what the Baker family prided themselves on? Doing what they loved and doing it well?

"Yes, but you knew that, too—"

"I do, and I'm done." Sharon jutted her chin.

"You said that already," Annie said wearily. "Done what?"

"Done settling," Sharon said. "I woke up one day and I just thought, another year has passed, I'm another year older, and I doubt your father has even noticed. I didn't want to wake up one year later feeling the same way."

Annie looked sadly at her mother. "But why didn't you explain to Dad—"

Sharon dismissed this with a wave of her hand. "Your father stopped noticing me years ago, Annie. Oh, he still loved me, at least that's what he said, but... Well, the sad truth of the matter is that sometimes love isn't enough."

Annie leaned back in her chair and stared out the window, on to the sidewalk that was filling with weekenders, people from Boston or its suburbs who were looking to take advantage of the unseasonably warm temperature. People who were in town for a bit of fun, rest, and relaxation. People whose world wasn't crashing down around them for the second time in their lives.

Annie wanted to tell her mother that she was being ridiculous and that they were going to sit down as a family and work this out.

But the other part of her knew that it wasn't her place. And that, worse, her mother had a point.

Because she knew more than anyone that sometimes love wasn't enough. No matter how badly you wished it could be.

The door opened, and a group of women came in, tourists from the way they looked around eagerly, and then chatted excitedly. Yes, it was a very cute café. Excellent food. Run by the lady in pink, Annie wanted to tell them.

Instead, she sighed and pushed back her chair. "I should let you get back to it. Val dropped my luggage off at the house, and I could use the walk."

"I'll see you at home," her mother told her. "We're closing up soon and Molly can cover the cleanup, that way you and I can talk some more."

"Honestly, Mom, all I want to do is crawl into bed and sleep." Even though it was three hours earlier on her internal clock, she'd been up since three thirty Seattle time to make her five-o'clock flight, and the events of the day had caught up with her. She was suddenly exhausted, so tired that she wasn't even sure she could handle the quarter-mile walk home, and even less sure of what would be waiting for her when she arrived.

An empty house. Hopefully not a pink one.

"There's plenty of food in the fridge," her mother said, sounding, for a brief, wonderful moment, like her old self. "And tomorrow night we'll have a big family dinner."

A family dinner. Without her father. Annie didn't know if she could make it out the door without crying, but somehow she did. She hadn't even bothered to bring up Sean; it seemed pointless in light of the bigger news. A real scoop, as Marcy would say.

Usually, when Annie visited, she liked to linger in town,

take in all the little shops and restaurants, and then sit by the harbor for a bit, watching the sailboats cut through the water in the distance. Today, though, she turned at the nearest corner and took a residential path home, stopping only once she'd reached the gravel driveway that led to the old rambling and rickety house, half-hidden by climbing roses and hydrangea come summertime.

But right now, it was in clear view, there, at the foot of the path, the cedar shingles weathered from time, the front planters overflowing with spring blooms.

Home sweet home.

So much for that.

Three

As much as Annie dreaded the thought of returning to the newspaper office, she also knew that it was the only way she was going to see her father.

Despite crawling into bed after a long, hot shower well before her usual bedtime, she slept late—something she decided to blame on the three-hour time difference, jet lag, and, let's face it, the train wreck that her life had become.

Telling herself that at least today she was prepared for the worst—and another Sean sighting—she pushed through the front door of the *Herald*, not at all surprised to see all the usual staff busy at their desks on a Saturday morning. It was the news, and even for a small-town paper like this one, it didn't stop.

At the kitchenette off the hallway, Marcy was poking her finger around in a box of donuts from the Bayview Bakery, and for once, Annie didn't feel the need to dodge her. If talking to her aunt meant that she could hide from Sean, then she'd happily put up with a little inquisition. That was the thing about Marcy; she was so easy to talk to. Too easy, really. People were drawn in by those wide eyes and sympathetic nods, the patient head tilt and clucks of disapproval at just the right time, and before anyone knew it, they had accidentally said too much and let something slip, and the next day, the entire town could read all about it in Marcy's Harmony Happenings column.

"Any glazed chocolates left?" Annie asked, doing a quick sweep down the hallway as she scooted over to Marcy at the counter. No Sean. She let out a breath she hadn't even realized she'd been holding.

Marcy must have caught it because she pursed her lips. "Sean probably beat me to it. He's not much of a gentleman, that fellow of yours."

At the mere mention of Sean, Annie's heart beat a little faster. She had hoped that he wouldn't be here today, that maybe he knew that this was her turf, her family business, and he'd respectfully stay away.

So much for that. When did Sean ever do anything that didn't suit him?

"Tell me about it," Annie said wryly. "But he's not my fellow anymore."

Hadn't been for a long time. And Marcy, of all people, knew that.

But Aunt Marcy just gave a little smile and said, "I wasn't sure if a reunion was in the cards."

Annie stared at her aunt, wondering if she was being hopeful in a loving way or if she was just fishing for her next hook. A reunion between her and her high-school-turned-college-sweetheart was far from possible, not that Annie would confirm or deny anything. Besides, she had someone else's personal life to discuss.

"Is it true that my father's been living here?" she asked.

Marcy might be the town gossip, but she was also extremely loyal to her only sibling and doted on her older brother as if he were still a child, not a man in his early sixties. Sure, she respected him as the editor of the paper, but that didn't stop her from making pastry runs when Mitch was working late or suggesting he take time off at the slightest hint of a winter cold.

The same devotion could be said for Annie's father, who patiently tolerated his sister's gossip column and her prying ways.

"Yes," she said with another sadder sigh. She pulled a jelly-stuffed donut from the box and took a hearty bite. "It feels treacherous to be eating this, what with where it came from and all. I'm surprised your father still supports your mother's side of the family."

Annie's aunt Kathy, her mother's younger sister, ran the best and only bakery in Harmony Cove, along with the adjacent Bayview Inn she owned with her husband. Her sweets were legendary on the Cape, and Marcy was one of her very best customers. At least, she used to be.

"Kathy's bakery is not only delicious but convenient. You don't want to have to drive to P-town for your sugar fix, do you?" Annie reached for a donut and then stopped herself. With the way things were going, Sean would catch her midbite, probably with sprinkles stuck to her lips.

Marcy seemed to consider this for a moment, allegiance

to her only sibling and access to her favorite sweets suddenly at odds.

"No, but I won't be adding to the tip jar for a while." Marcy huffed and took another bite of her donut, licking the strawberry jelly off her bottom lip. "So, you've seen your mother."

Annie nodded. She would neither confirm nor deny how she felt about her mother's new look.

"It's quite the talk of the town," Marcy said with a raise of her eyebrows.

Annie wasn't sure if her aunt was referring to the big split or the new look, so she remained silent.

"Your mother was always such a natural beauty," Marcy mused. Her eyes narrowed behind her glasses. "Until her sister got her hands on her."

And there it was. Annie should have known that her mother's older sister, Sandra, might have had something to do with this. After years of being the only divorced sister and trolling the singles scene on her own, she finally had a sidekick.

"It's certainly...different" was all Annie said. Then, "And that's off the record."

"Of course," Marcy said with a little smile. They both knew that nothing was off the record when it came to Marcy's column. Except for her brother, that was.

Annie looked properly at her aunt, who was still enjoying her morning treat, and probably not her first. "I'm worried about Dad. Is he going to be okay?"

"I don't know, dear," Marcy said with a slow shake of her head. "I keep hoping that things will settle down, but despite my sources, I'm not privy to what goes on behind closed doors, and so long as your mother struts around town looking like a middle-aged Barbie doll, I'm taking that as a sign that things won't be resolved anytime soon."

Annie chewed her lip, replaying everything her mother had said in the café, just as she had all of yesterday until she'd finally worn herself out and fallen into a fitful but, mercifully, dreamless sleep while the sun was still up.

"I'll talk to her. I'm here for a week," she said firmly.

"If anyone can help, it's you, dear," Marcy said, though she didn't sound hopeful.

"Anything else I've missed?" Annie asked.

"Well..."

Annie's eyes popped as her heart dropped like a stone. "I didn't mean that seriously! Do you mean there's *more*?"

"Oh, honey." Marcy chuckled softly. "There's always more. And I suppose you may as well hear it from me."

That was Marcy's favorite motto, the one she justified to let everyone know everything about everyone else.

"Yes," Annie said, bracing herself. "I suppose I may as well."

"Your cousin Hillary is engaged," Marcy said simply.

"Oh." Annie hadn't even known that Hillary was seriously dating anyone. The last time she'd visited, Hillary was still complaining about how difficult it was to meet men she hadn't either kissed in the sandbox, kissed in middle school, or never wanted to kiss—ever.

"To Tim Reynolds," Marcy deadpanned. She took an extra-slow bite of her donut, eyeing Annie steadily through her thick glasses while that news sank in.

And news it was.

"Hillary is marrying *Tim*?" Annie stared at her aunt, horrified. She couldn't have been more shocked than if, say, her mother had decided to up and leave her father. "*Tim* Tim? *Caroline's* Tim?"

"Yep. This June," Marcy added, a whisper of a smile flitting over her mouth as she went in for the final bite of her donut.

That soon? And her mother and sisters hadn't said a word!

"I thought he was in Boston," Annie said, trying to make sense of this information.

"He moved back, along with his brother." Marcy shrugged. "Seems to be a trend lately. Certainly adds some interest to things."

Annie wouldn't call Tim Reynolds resurfacing interesting. She'd call it unfortunate. And ominous.

"Does Caroline know?" Annie could only imagine how her sister would take the news that her ex-fiancé was now marrying their cousin. And not just any cousin, but Caroline's favorite cousin. Caroline's best friend.

Marcy shrugged. "Unlike you, Caroline never visits. She hasn't shown her face in town since... Well, you know."

Yes, they all knew. The entire town knew. Possibly all of Cape Cod, given the newspaper, and therefore Harmony Happenings's distribution reach.

Caroline had been happily engaged to her high school sweetheart, had planned a beautiful wedding, right down to the smallest details, had Aunt Sandra design a stunning hand-beaded dress with a tulle veil, and had Aunt Kathy build a four-layer cake complete with buttercream flowers that matched her bouquets. She'd dared to risk an outdoor reception because she didn't think even the clouds would dare to threaten the day—and they hadn't. It was a clear blue sky, the perfect late spring morning, and the happiest day of Caroline's life. They'd all gotten ready together in their childhood home, in Caroline's blue bedroom, before excitedly climbing into the limos—their first time!—to arrive at the church where all of their friends and family had already gathered. The bridal party waited, the anticipation electrifying, for the remaining guests to filter in and the cue for the procession to begin. But the knock on the door wasn't from the Kathy, who was stationed to let everyone know when they should come out, but instead, from Tim's brother, Lucas, telling them in no uncertain terms that Tim was a no-show.

"I rarely talk to Caroline," Annie murmured. It wasn't that they were on bad terms, only that they were both busy with their careers. "It's been three years since…" She still couldn't bring herself to say it. "Maybe she won't care."

But she knew that was wishful thinking. There was a reason that Caroline didn't come back to Harmony Cove and that reason was Tim Reynolds.

Marcy dabbed the corners of her mouth with a napkin and said, "You'd know best, wouldn't you, dear?"

Annie pulled in a breath and pinched her mouth, scolding herself for getting dragged into this conversation and knowing better than to say another word.

She left her aunt to help herself to another donut and went in search of her father, her entire reason for being at the office today. With any luck, she'd get in and get out without seeing Sean.

But as she rounded the corner, she didn't just see Sean, more like she bulldozed straight into his chest.

"Oh." She fumbled back, feeling her cheeks burn as she stared up into those deep-set dark eyes that seemed to bore right through her. His mouth quirked ever so slightly, as if he found this amusing, or easy. Or...pleasurable. Well, it wasn't. "I'm—looking for my father."

Not exactly the first words she imagined saying to him if she ever spoke to him again, but then, they were in public, and profanity had no business in the workplace.

"He's not in," Sean said without a hint of emotion.

Nice of Marcy to mention that.

Annie craned her neck to glance back around the corner, only to see that her aunt had moved in closer as she clutched a glazed donut, no doubt eager to overhear their conversation.

Sean took stock of the situation before motioning her into the nearest office with a tip of his head. Annie hesitated but saw no choice. It was this or face Marcy again, and she suspected that this time her aunt wasn't going to let her go so easily.

Sean closed the door behind him, leaving Annie with a moment to take in her surroundings. It was her office, she realized with a start, the one that looked out over the back of the building. She used to love staring down into the gardens each spring and fall to watch the colors bloom and change. Her desk—now his—was rearranged, with the computer set on an angle in the right corner instead of centered, the way she preferred. Her houseplant was still alive, largely in part to Marcy, no doubt, who talked to all the office plants, filling them in on all the happenings in town. Her photos were gone, her diploma, too, and in their place were framed prints of the harbor, no doubt painted by a local artist.

She'd loved this office, and now Sean had gone and messed it all up, just like everything else he touched.

Sean sat down in her chair. The one she'd picked out at the furniture store in Chatham with her father on her very first official day of work, right after graduating from UMass. Back then, Sean was still working as an intern because he started grad school in the fall.

Annie didn't sit in the visitor's chair, and not just because it would feel too strange to do so. She intended to keep this brief. Marcy didn't spend all day in the office; she liked to be out and about, lending an ear to anyone with a story to tell or a problem to unload.

"Is my father coming back soon?" she asked, struggling to look in Sean's direction and not only because he had made himself at home in her space.

He looked good. Too good. The years had been kind to him, turning his boyish looks more manly, accentuating his jawline, the sincerity in his eyes when he smiled, and turning his once-lanky figure muscular.

"He's golfing with the mayor," Sean replied.

In other words, he'd be gone all morning, and longer if they stayed through lunch. "I should go, then," she said, moving toward the door.

"Wait—" Sean's voice was so insistent that Annie was forced to turn back and face him.

She glared at him, forcing herself to stay strong, challenging him to say whatever was so pressing, and wishing that she didn't care so much what it might be.

"It's...nice to see you again, Annie," he said, his eyes softening as he stared at her.

For a moment she let herself get lost in his face, the one that she had memorized, the one that she once longed to gaze at more than any other. It was her favorite face, her favorite smile. She knew every freckle, every eyelash, the small cleft of his chin and the slight bump of his nose. The feel of his skin under her fingertips. The warmth of his body. The comfort of his touch.

Darn if that didn't feel good to hear. If a part of her didn't need him to care. To miss her. Maybe even to still want her.

But she did not want him, she reminded herself, standing a little straighter. And she hadn't missed him for a long time, not since the tears dried up.

She gave a curt nod and turned the door handle. "Well, I have to get to work. I'm in town on an assignment. I'm covering the *Herald*'s anniversary. The paper is turning one hundred this week."

She hadn't even had a chance to tell her father this yet. It was meant to be a big surprise, but right now, the surprise was for her, and if she and her father were going to be discussing anything, it was the state of his marriage.

Sean's eyebrows rose as he leaned back in *her* wooden banker's chair and then pitched it forward. She had sort of been hoping he'd fall squarely on his backside.

"I'm covering that story, too."

She didn't think she could narrow her eyes further, but she somehow managed. "You? Why?"

He shrugged. "It's the paper's anniversary. Shouldn't we cover it?"

She didn't like his use of the word *we*, as if he had any relationship to her family's paper. "Yes, but you? Of all people?"

Meaning the guy who had made it very clear that this paper and this town would never be enough for him—when it was everything to her father?

"Well, it was me or Marcy," Sean said with a light laugh. He stopped when he saw that she was far from amused. "Your father's being featured in the article, so an objective lens was needed."

"Objective. That's an interesting take for a story with so much…heart." She tipped her head, feeling her lips curl. "But then, last I checked, you didn't have one of those."

"Annie." Sean sighed. "Can we talk?"

"There's nothing to talk about," she said, swinging the door wide open, letting him know that anything he said now would be broadcast as far as the Vineyard.

Sure enough, he hesitated, his eyes flitting from the papers on his desk and back to her.

From a few feet down the hall, Annie heard a shuffle of feet, and then a fake fig tree in the corner started to sway.

"We can talk about the article," he said. "We're both covering the same story. And I have some good scoop you might be interested in hearing."

"I'm sure that my father can provide all the information I need to know about his family's paper," she said pointedly, closing the door again now that she was aware of Marcy's vicinity.

"Not everything. I'm keeping some things a surprise for my article." Sean's eyes locked hers in a challenge.

Annie's entire body felt like it was vibrating. She wanted to call his bluff, to tell him she'd be fine on her own, but then she thought of what was at stake, and what she'd already lost, thanks to him.

She needed this article to be more than a success. She needed it to be unforgettable.

"Fine," she said, hoping her tone was breezier than she felt about the possibility of spending even five more minutes in his company.

They were both professionals, and he had proven that he was always willing to put his career above all else.

Maybe it was time for her to do the same. Even if her heart wasn't in it.

Sean didn't have anything to share with Annie that she wouldn't already know. The Bakers were a tightknit family, and this newspaper was her legacy—or it had been until she decided to walk away from it.

That had come as a surprise.

"So, how's Seattle treating you?" he asked conversationally as they stepped outside—his idea, under the excuse to get away from Marcy, who was about five seconds away from holding a glass to his door, but the truth was that he felt restless and nervous around Annie. He didn't like the tension between them any more than he enjoyed the silence these past few years.

He'd missed her from the moment that he drove over the town line and hopped the ferry to Boston Harbor, knowing that he'd given up a life he loved and a girl he loved, but that he'd had no other choice.

"Coffee?" he asked, motioning to the Sweet Harmony Café up ahead. Once, it had been their place, his home away from home, where they'd hang out after school on rainy days, or later, work on research together in those college years when they were both interning at the *Herald* during the summer.

Annie hesitated and then said, "I suppose you've seen my mother since you've been back."

Only from afar, but Sean knew what she was referring to, of course. Sharon was clearly trying out a new look for this next phase of her life. News of the separation had come as a surprise to him, too. He'd always seen the Bakers as a solid couple, and a happy one, certainly happier than his own parents ever were.

"I was very sorry to hear about their marriage," he said gently, but she bristled at the sympathy he offered.

They weren't close anymore, he reminded himself. He wasn't the one she turned to, and he hadn't been in a long time.

"We can go somewhere else if you'd like." Harmony Cove was full of quaint restaurants and coffee shops, but that only helped the businesses rather than create competition. There were plenty of tourists that flocked to the town every spring through fall to more than fill every table.

Usually, by the winter, the locals were relieved when the first snowfall hit and the traffic slowed.

"Why don't you just tell me what you have for the article," Annie said, stopping to drop onto a bench near the harbor.

"Actually, I was thinking that we might collaborate on the article," Sean said. Then, recalling what she'd said earlier in his office, and trying his best not to take offense to it, he added, "Share the facts, I mean."

"I don't need your help to write an article about my family business," Annie told him. "And I certainly don't need help from someone who up until quite recently thought that he was too good for it."

"Hey, you left, too," he shot back, kicking himself when he did. It was a defense mechanism, a knee-jerk reaction because she made his decision to leave this town sound so simple when it was anything but that.

She stared at him, allowing him to take in her face for a moment, the full lips that he had once kissed, so easily, so naturally. The blue eyes, as dark and deep as the ocean when you looked out on to the horizon, now seemed to pierce right through him, seeing him for what he was.

But not who he wanted to be.

"I did leave," Annie said. "But that's because my father encouraged me to. He thought it would be good for me to go out into the world and make a name for myself outside of the family paper."

"And have you?" Damn. Again, he'd said the wrong thing. He knew firsthand just how proud Mitch Baker was of his daughter.

"I'm up for a big promotion," Annie replied with a lift of her chin and a satisfied smirk.

He raised his eyebrows, both impressed, surprised, and admittedly disappointed. The reality that things had changed in his absence hit him with full force. Annie had moved away and moved on. And soon she'd be gone again.

And he'd have no one to blame but himself.

"Congrats," he managed. "Not that I'm surprised. You're your father's daughter."

Annie cleared her throat. "How about you? What could have possibly made you give up your big, prestigious reporting gig to come back to this small-town newspaper that doesn't even have a regional circulation?"

"I had a change of heart," he said simply.

Now she stared at him, one eyebrow slightly lifted, her lips twitching, as if she was fighting off a laugh.

"You had a change of heart," she repeated. "You suddenly decided that hard news wasn't working for you and that you'd be better off here, at the *Harmony Herald*, where the biggest story is usually about the national weather?"

"Hey, hurricanes are a big deal," Sean said good-naturedly, but there was an ache forming in his chest that he couldn't ignore.

Annie continued to stare at him and then leaned back against the bench, her gaze returning to the harbor. "I don't buy it."

And rightfully so.

"Is it so strange to think that after all these years, I wanted to come home?" Sean asked, hoping that she wasn't half the reporter that he knew she was.

Annie kept her eyes on a sailboat that was gliding through the water, the wind pushing it at a steady speed.

"I guess my real question is...why now?" she finally said.

When she turned to look at him this time, her eyes were dark with hurt, and he opened his mouth to explain and then stopped himself. There was nothing that he could say that could change what he'd done. He'd left her, put his career ahead of their plans, their future, and their love.

"Well, I guess you didn't have a change of heart about me," she said with a little shake of her head. "Or you would have come back much sooner."

"You knew I always wanted to make a name for myself," he said. They both did. They wanted to feel important, like they could make a difference.

"You wanted to be remembered for your voice," she reminded him. "For telling stories that mattered."

"Doesn't every reporter?" he countered. "Don't you?"

Annie paused for a moment, perhaps because he'd touched upon something, but then fired back, "You don't need to be reporting from the front line to matter."

He saw the hurt in her eyes, heard the defensive tone of her voice, and could only nod because he agreed with her. Mitch Baker may not have traveled the globe or covered foreign affairs but what he wrote about had a direct impact on the community.

And on Sean.

Try telling that to his father, Sean thought bitterly. Contrary to what Annie might think, it was Bill Morrison who had kept Sean from ever wanting to return to this town all these years, after he'd done such a good job of running him out of it.

His career was all Sean had for the last six years. The only thing he cared about—or allowed himself to care about.

Until now.

The wounds were reopened, all the hurt coming back in, and everywhere he went in this town, he was reminded of what he'd once had and had given up. Of what he'd lost and still stood to lose.

"Are you telling me that you're perfectly content to be working at the *Harmony Herald*?" Annie tipped her head.

"Yes," Sean said, because he was. More than content. He was relieved. Nearly happy—but that wasn't possible at the moment, given his current situation and reason for being back in town. Maybe it never would be again.

"I grew up at that paper. We both did," he said, giving her a smile. "It feels like...home."

"*My* home," she told him firmly, her gaze flashing with anger when she turned to face him. "And you're sitting in *my* office."

"You left. You're just visiting," he reminded her. Even though he wished that weren't true.

"And, what, you're here to stay?"

Sean swallowed hard. "For now. I'm here now."

She gave a knowing smile, one that hit him right where it hurt the most. "What could be so important here that wasn't six years ago? Why is this town good enough now but it wasn't then?"

Sean's heart was pounding, and he opened his mouth to tell her the truth—every last detail—but then he stopped himself. His purpose for being back in Harmony Cove was separate from his feelings for Annie—just like his reason for leaving.

"It was always enough," he said quietly, reaching out a hand, longing to touch her fingers, her arm, her hair, anything. Before he could make contact, he thought better of it and pulled back.

Time had passed. They'd gone their separate ways. And now, like before, they still weren't in one place.

"Look," he said, clearing his throat. "I want to do right by your father with this article. He's put his entire life into that paper and his family's legacy, and this is the one time he'll be honored for the work he's done. How he's impacted this town. Inspired people. I know he inspired me."

He thought he saw Annie soften a bit.

"We both want the same thing," he pressed. They always did, he wanted to add, but again, he knew that it was useless. "I can write the article on my own, but it would be a lot better with your insight. You know your father better than anyone. Would you be willing to do that? Work with me? One last time?"

"For my father," Annie said after a beat, and, it would seem, with an extreme lack of enthusiasm. "You know I'd do anything for him."

"And I feel the same. You know I love your dad," Sean said, placing a hand on his chest. Mitch Baker was more than a surrogate father to him. He was the father he'd always wished he had.

And he might have been family if Sean's own hadn't gotten in the way.

"We can divide and conquer, chat with the locals, hear their favorite stories and memories," Sean suggested, if only to make it easier for Annie. He owed her that much.

"Well, my article is due a week from Monday," Annie said.

"Mine is running in next Sunday's edition," Sean replied. "That gives us a full week."

One week. To write an article that was somehow worthy of the man who had made Sean want to be better and do better. To write something he'd be proud of—and maybe his own father would be, too.

And one week to spend with Annie.

Before life pulled them apart again.

Four

When her mother said she wanted a family dinner, Annie imagined them all gathered around the big farmhouse table. Sharon, however, had other ideas.

Annie struggled to keep up with her mom's new, brisk pace as they approached the center of town, all of its shops closed for the day and the light from the restaurants glowing through the lead-paned windows. Even the cobblestone roads couldn't stop Sharon from hurrying across the intersection in heels that must have been purchased at Sandra's boutique—or borrowed from Sandra herself. Even in her sensible flats, Annie worried about twisting an ankle on the uneven surface, but her mother's determined stride didn't waver. Annie slowed down only when they passed the building of the *Herald*, where, sure enough, a lamp flicked on in the upstairs window.

It wasn't unusual for Annie's father to be working late. If anything, it was more common than not. But somehow knowing that he wasn't sitting at his desk putting the finishing touches on tomorrow's edition, but rather, heating a bowl of ramen in the staff microwave or pouring a bowl of cereal and carrying it up the back winding stairs to the small three-room apartment on the top floor whose sole purpose until now was for storing copies of old papers, made her heart fill with a sadness so deep that she had to stop walking for a moment.

Her mother, however, took no pause and maybe no notice.

"Hurry up, Annie!" she called gaily from the next corner. "The ladies are all waiting for us!"

By ladies, Sharon was referring to their extended family, which was indeed comprised largely of women. There was Marcy on Annie's father's side, of course, who had never married or had children, and then Annie's mother's two sisters who lived here on the Cape—Sandra, the eldest, and Kathy, the baby, who each had three daughters. Their brother and his two daughters all lived in New York and didn't make it back to Harmony Cove often.

Two of Sandra's children were twins, though not identical. Some even thought that Annie looked more like her cousin Kayla than Phoebe did, but Annie didn't see the resemblance. She knew she had her father's eyes. Last Annie knew, Kayla was living abroad, but considering the revelations of the past twenty-four hours, this might have changed. Kathy's daughter Paige lived in Boston, though she often came to the Cape on weekends. The rest of Annie's cousins had all stayed in town and she was very much looking forward to seeing them, along with Molly and Valerie, who wouldn't miss an evening out. She had yet to see Valerie since being dropped off at the *Herald* yesterday, and she had some words for that sister.

"You didn't want to host everyone?" Annie asked once she'd caught up to her mother.

"Kathy needs the business," Sharon said simply, which did its job of silencing Annie, whether it was the truth or not. The Bayview Inn included the cozy waterfront restaurant mostly run by Kathy's husband, and during warmer months, its patio was always filled with tourists and locals, happy to linger at a table, enjoying drinks and Uncle Joe's mouth-watering crabcakes while watching the sun set over Cape Cod Bay. Tonight, though, it was too chilly of a night to rely on heat lamps, which meant that between the three families in attendance, they'd be taking up a good portion of the dimly lit restaurant.

"We're going to need a private room to house us all," Annie pointed out, knowing that the Bayview Bistro offered no such accommodations.

"Nonsense." Sharon looked unfazed. "We're going to sit in the bar area, of course! That's where all the action is!"

"By action, please don't tell me you mean men," Annie said.

"You never know if Sean might stop in," her mother said suggestively. "You haven't told me how you feel about him being back in town."

"A little warning would have been nice," Annie said. About a lot of things. "I've seen him at the newspaper, but I can't imagine he would show up here, knowing that it's our family hangout."

Her mother just shrugged gleefully. "He's been into the café, so you never know!"

Annie could only hope that her mother was wrong. With newfound dread, she followed her mother to the side of the historic inn to where they could directly enter the restaurant without crossing through the lobby. Annie watched her mother shimmy the tight, hot pink skirt around her hips, fluff her hair, and open the door, wondering just who this creature was and what she had done with her mother.

Her wonderful, grounded, perfectly content mother, who loved nothing more than gathering all of the birds in her nest, as she liked to say. To host her loved ones around the big farmhouse table in their ancestral home, and serve cherished dishes made with ingredients fresh from her garden. Annie had dared to think she might taste a slice of her mother's delicious berry crumble tonight, complete with her homemade ice cream.

She supposed she'd just have to go to the café and order it like all the other people in town.

With a heavy sigh, Annie followed her mother straight to the bar, which was crowded and noisy as usual for a Saturday night, confirming her suspicions that Kathy and Joe had no shortage of business. Her eyes darted over the crowd as she held her breath, but a quick assessment showed no signs of Sean, his brother, or any of his known friends. She relaxed even further when her gaze landed on her aunt Kathy, standing at the polished wood bar, chatting with one of the young female bartenders in that friendly, maternal way of hers.

Annie and Kathy had always been close, maybe because Kathy was more than five years younger than her mother and, well, not her mother. Kathy would be frank with her. She'd put a stop to this nonsense.

"Annie!" Kathy spotted her across the room and, abandoning her drink, hurried through the crowd to greet her. She opened her arms wide and pulled Annie into a much-needed and wonderfully familiar embrace.

Annie closed her eyes and sank into the hug, needing it more than she even knew.

"What the heck is happening?" Annie whispered into her aunt's ear, hearing the desperation in her voice.

Kathy pulled her back and widened her dark eyes—a look that conveyed a hundred words that didn't need to be spoken. Meaning, Kathy saw it. Kathy got it. Kathy agreed.

"I've been so anxious about you coming back," Kathy said urgently, taking Annie by the elbow and leading her to the corner of the bar. "I had to wrestle that phone from my own hand at least a hundred times to stop myself from telling you the news."

"Why didn't you?" Annie cried, in a stage-whisper, of course.

"I didn't want to worry you!" Then, with a look of resignation, she said, "And I guess I hoped that things would all blow over by the time you visited."

Given how infrequently that was, Annie understood Kathy's logic. And optimism.

"My mom said that she kicked my dad out in *September*! On their *wedding anniversary*!" Annie pulled her aunt deeper into the corner, even though she was fairly confident that every person in this room—except for the few lone tourists—was already well aware of the Baker family drama.

Kathy nodded in confirmation and bit down on her lower lip. "Yep."

"And the new look? When did this start?" Annie asked.

"Not long afterward," Kathy said, positively ravaging that lip now.

"And this family gathering? I love coming here, but Mom is using it as an excuse not to host one of her big family meals," Annie said. And Annie counted on them.

"I miss those family meals," Kathy groaned. "Those marinated vegetables. Her signature lasagna! Her bread. I'm a baker, and I can't even knead like she does, which is why I mostly stick to cakes and cookies. And can we talk about her—"

"Berry crumble?" Annie and Kathy both cried in unison and then, both slumping in disappointment, fell silent.

"She loves throwing those parties. She loves having a full house!" Annie said. But then, she supposed that her mother loved her dad once, too. And that had come to an end.

Her eyes prickled and she blinked quickly, trying to compose herself lest the Baker family make a bigger public scene than it already was.

"Oh, honey, don't cry," Kathy pleaded, grabbing Annie by the wrist. "At least, not here."

Annie managed to laugh. Leave it to Kathy to always make her smile.

"Your mother's been...getting out more," Kathy said delicately, but again with the eyes. They went wide, they didn't blink, and oh, they said everything that Annie needed to hear.

And didn't want to know.

"Dating?" Annie almost screamed at the thought of it.

"Well...more like...*browsing*?" Kathy blurted and then quickly pulled Annie in for another hug before she could react. She squeezed her tight. "Oh, I'm so glad that you're back. You're my favorite, you know. Of all the nieces." She winked at Annie after letting her go.

Given that Kathy had nine of them, that was saying something.

"I know," Annie said, feeling another smile pull at her face.

"Remember, I'm here for you," Kathy said, giving her a pat of encouragement as they joined the group.

It was a small comfort, but one that Annie appreciated, maybe even more than her aunt knew.

She hugged all of her cousins, commenting on their clothes, asking about their jobs, and, of course, their love lives. Paige hadn't made it for the evening—she was still in Boston, still dating the same guy she'd been with for years with no plans in sight, which Annie knew worried Kathy to no end. Kathy's other daughters couldn't make it, either: Emily was home with her young daughter, and Lucy was putting the finishing touches on a cake order at the bakery and would be over soon. Sandra's twins let her know that they were both single, one hopeful, one not so much.

And then there was Hillary.

"I hear that wedding bells are in order," Annie said to Hillary, and couldn't help but again catch the suggestive look from Kathy from across the table, who no doubt had *plenty* of thoughts on this subject. There was no way that one of Kathy's daughters would have swooped in on the man who had ceremoniously crushed Caroline's heart, but then, this family wasn't what Annie had once thought it was, was it?

"I'm having an engagement party on Friday," Hillary said hopefully. "Aunt Kathy is hosting it at the inn. If you're still in town, I'd love for you to come."

Annie would still be in town, and the way she saw it, she'd have to attend, even if it made her feel traitorous to do so.

She wanted to ask how this had happened. Hillary and Tim Reynolds, of all people?

Normally she would ask her mother, but her judgment couldn't be trusted these days. Kathy might fill her in if she stopped by the bakery. Although, did she even want to know the dirty details? And would it change anything?

She moved on to her sisters, accepting a glass of wine from Valerie in the process.

"Why didn't you two tell me?" she demanded, her eyes flitting from Molly to Valerie and back again.

Molly shifted guiltily on her feet and stared at the floor, but Val just tipped her head and said, "Which part?"

Annie forced herself not to smile. Only Val could make light of such personal disasters and get away with it.

"Let's start with Mom and Dad. Are they getting a divorce?" she hissed, cringing just hearing the words come out of her mouth.

Molly looked like she might cry, and Val's mouth settled into a firm line. "I don't know," she said. "Dad doesn't want to talk about it, and Mom seems to have forgotten that Dad even exists."

"But they must see each other?" Annie pointed out.

Val and Molly exchanged a look. They both shook their heads.

"What? But how is that possible? This is a small town!" Annie struggled to lower her voice, not wanting to draw any attention from her mother, who was laughing with Sandra at the bar.

"Dad's been living at the office, not that that's anything new," Val said, referring to his long days that often extended into long nights.

"He's stopped eating lunch at the café, and well, you know Dad, he's not one to go out much," Molly added.

"Neither is Mom, but I get the feeling that's changed," Annie said darkly, casting her mother a fleeting look in time to see her tipping back a shot. A shot!

"Oh, yes. That's *definitely* changed," Valerie nodded. "She's a regular at all the local hot spots, as she calls them. Sandra's so happy to have a buddy, they must be out two, three times a week."

Again, Molly seemed on the brink of tears. Annie was close to it herself. It was no secret that Sandra, who had been single for most of her adult life after a brief and disastrous marriage, was forever on the lookout for love. The thought of their mother saddling up next to Sandra at noisy bars and drinking shots (shots!) was an image that Annie couldn't get used to just yet. And hoped that she never would.

Like Kathy had said, there was hope that this would all just blow over.

"What about the holidays?" Annie asked, knowing how much her family treasured their traditions. "They must have gotten together for Christmas!"

Valerie shook her head. "Dad was with Marcy. We spent the day with Aunt Kathy and Uncle Joe here at the inn. Sandra was spending it with the Reynoldses, seeing as they're about to become family."

Annie closed her eyes briefly. This just got worse and worse. "Does Caroline know yet?"

"Nope," Valerie affirmed. "But she will. I mean, she can't avoid coming back to town forever, can she?"

Probably not. After all, even Sean had come back eventually.

"Okay, let's discuss Sean. Back in town. Working at the paper?" Annie stared at Val, hoping that she could maybe explain what Sean had failed to do earlier that day. Oh, he'd confirmed he was back all right, but he was yet to give a good reason why.

"Why don't you ask him yourself?" Val said with a teasing grin. "He's sitting right behind you."

"What?" Annie felt her cheeks blanch and she studied her sister's face, trying to read it, hoping that the glee she saw pass through Valerie's eyes meant that she'd gotten the reaction she'd hoped for and that her little joke was well played.

Because certainly it was a joke. It had to be.

Except...Molly looked like she wanted to turn and run. Meaning that Val wasn't joking, but simply basking in someone else's drama.

Or misfortune.

Her sister casually sipped her wine, and subtly, Annie

tossed her hair over her shoulder and took a quick peek, her entire body seeming to shudder when she saw Sean sitting at a high-top near the window with his cousin Travis, looking just as handsome as he had earlier in the day, still wearing the same clothes, his shirtsleeves now rolled up. Either he hadn't seen her yet or he was choosing to ignore her.

She had to assume it was the latter. It was impossible not to notice the Baker, Stewart, and Ross women, who were occupying half the bar and two small tables.

Heck, it was impossible not to notice just her mother these days.

"Sean moved back to town because his mother's sick," Molly said matter-of-factly, bringing Annie straight back to the present.

"Oh." Annie felt a cold wash over her. She'd always liked Sean's mother, and she knew that she was Sean's preferred parent, too. And if her illness was enough to bring Sean back to town, then the prognosis couldn't be good. Recalling the words she'd thrown at him this morning, she felt sick with remorse.

Darn it, she thought, taking a long sip of her wine. It was so much easier when Sean was the jerk, and not her.

∽

"Was that Annie Baker I just saw at the bar?" Travis asked as he came back to the table holding two beers.

Sean wasted no time in reaching for his. He cut a glance across the room, where, sure enough, Annie, two of her sisters, and half her cousins and aunts (save Marcy, thankfully) were laughing and having a good time.

He couldn't help but feel a pang—of jealousy, or longing. He couldn't tell. He'd loved being a part of that family —the big dinners around the old farm table or out back on the porch in the warmer months. The holidays gathered around the crackling fire, Annie's sisters quietly reading or playing a board game, and Sharon in the kitchen, making a feast.

He looked away and cleared his throat, and then took a long sip of his beer, which didn't go down easily. He should have known better than to agree to come here. The Bayview Inn was owned by Annie's aunt and this restaurant was a popular gathering place, meaning the risk of Annie being here was high and he knew it. And deep down maybe he wanted this. To see her again.

Because it sure beat avoiding her.

His emotions were all over the place since he'd gotten the call that resulted in him giving notice to his long-time employer and moving back to Harmony Cove, and they'd wreaked even more havoc since he first saw Annie again. He wasn't used to this tightness in his chest, and he didn't like it. For the past six years, he'd kept his emotions at bay, reporting on stories with facts from a purely objective lens, detaching himself from the pain of his subjects, the unthinkable horror that some of them recanted—or that he witnessed firsthand. It was the only way to keep going.

The only way to never look back.

But here he was. And so, it would seem, was Annie.

"She's visiting for the week," he told his cousin, hoping

his tone was casual enough to show that he wasn't bothered, that he didn't care.

But the tightness in his chest told him what he already knew. He did care. He'd never stopped.

Travis had been in the same grade as him growing up, and they made a point of meeting for drinks once a week since Sean's return to town. Sean felt closer to him than he ever did his own brother, who wasn't just older by two years but opposite in every possible way, and with Travis being an only child, the feeling was mutual.

"So you've spoken?" Travis looked surprised at this possibility.

"She stopped by the paper," Sean said, glancing over at the bar and then away before Annie caught his stare. He didn't want to make things awkward. He was here to blow off steam, not stir up bad feelings.

"And how'd that go?" Travis asked, leaning forward. The gleam in his eyes underscored his amusement at Sean's expense.

"Oh, you know..." Tense. Awkward. Downright shocking, until it faded into resignation and then sadness. He'd seen Annie again, after all these years. There was no bright smile like she used to toss his way every time he'd pull into her driveway to pick her up for a date. No hug. Certainly no kiss.

Not even a handshake, not that he'd have wanted that.

He didn't know what he'd been expecting, but not this distance that was worse than any physical space. Not this feeling that they were strangers. That time hadn't made their breakup any easier for her than it had been for him.

"You've seen her, though, over the years," Sean said, and his cousin nodded. Once, Sean would have avoided the burning question, but tonight, he had to ask. "Do you... know if she's seeing anyone?"

"Not that I know of." Travis set down his beer and turned the glass in his hands. "But I haven't seen her in over a year. I might have heard her mention a guy in Seattle once, but no one's ever come home with her, if that's what you're asking. But if you want to know, why don't you just ask Marcy?"

Sean laughed even as his gut burned. A guy in Seattle. There hadn't been any other girl for him in all these years. He hadn't made time for a relationship and hadn't stuck around in one place long enough, not even his home base of DC. He was always on the move, chasing another lead, following the next big story.

But now, well, he didn't have an excuse, did he?

His gaze wandered over to Annie again, knowing that he did have an excuse. How could he move on with another woman when his heart still belonged to the one across the room—who wouldn't even look at him?

"What about you?" he asked Travis, knowing full well that his cousin hadn't been in a serious relationship in his entire life.

"What about me?" Travis grinned. "Summer's almost here. And you know what that means."

"Tourists." Sean didn't need to be told. Once, summer had been his favorite season, when he and Annie would ride their bikes out to the shore, spread out their towels on the warm sand, and cool off in the salty water.

"You'll be here this summer," Travis said. "I'll get you back out there."

Would he be here this summer? Sean's stomach shifted with unease, as it always did when he thought of his mother and her health, which was failing by the day. He didn't want to think of a day when she wouldn't be a part of his life, but he also knew that he had to brace himself for it. Plan for it.

Just like he knew that he couldn't ignore the fact that his position was being held for him, and that his office back in DC was there and waiting.

"I'll be busy working," Sean said wryly. But where? If his father had it his way, Sean would be on the first ferry out after his mother's funeral.

He swallowed back another sip of beer, not wanting to picture that.

A burst of laughter rose from across the room, and Sean's attention was pulled to the bar again, where Annie and her family were all raising glasses of pink champagne in some sort of toast.

A celebration. It was nice to see.

Because contrary to what Annie believed, all he'd ever wanted was for her to be happy.

"I think I'll get us another round," Travis suddenly said.

Sean tapped the side of his glass. "The glass is more than half full."

"That's so optimistic of you." Travis pushed off his stool. "Hold on to that thought."

Before Sean could argue, his cousin was gone, heading toward the bar.

Just as Annie was walking toward him.

"Hey," Annie said, giving Sean a small smile. It hurt, the action, however simple, because it no longer felt easy, and because giving in and showing some level of connection just stirred up all that hurt and pain, and brought down the walls that she had so purposefully constructed, protecting her from him.

Now she was forced to recognize the connection they once shared. To relive some of those memories. To admit that he once meant something to her and that on some level, however unwanted, he still did.

"Hey." Sean looked confused as she slid onto Travis's seat, all too aware that every one of her family members was watching her right now and would soon be talking about her, too.

At least Marcy wasn't here. Unless she was hiding behind a plant—it wouldn't be the first time.

"I heard about your mom," she said, hearing her voice thicken with emotion. She didn't even know the diagnosis, but she knew it had to be serious to bring Sean back to town. To pull him from such a prestigious job.

To bring him back to their lowly small-town paper.

He nodded his head, silent for a moment, and when he spoke, he didn't look her in the eyes. "Thanks."

It was a side of him that she'd seen only once before, the day that he told her he was taking the job in DC.

"You know I always liked your mom," Annie said. She still saw her around, before she moved to Seattle, and on the occasional visit, at the café, or just walking through town.

Debbie Morrison always stopped to greet her with a hug, ask how she was doing, and then give her a long, apologetic look that made Annie quickly make up an excuse about needing to be somewhere, even if she had nowhere to go at all.

Now, Annie wished that she hadn't always run off so quickly. She stared into Sean's dark eyes, wondering if he'd open up and tell her what she both longed to know and feared to hear.

Instead, he said nothing, reminding her that they were not close anymore.

And they hadn't been for a very long time.

"I take it that this is what brought you back to town," Annie said.

Sean only nodded.

Annie sighed, bracing herself for what she was about to say even as she knew that it had to be done.

"Look, it's been a long time. We've both moved on," she said, glancing up at him, wondering if this were true. Did he have a girlfriend? She wouldn't know. Didn't want to know really.

Definitely shouldn't care.

"I'm only in town for a week, and next time I visit, there's no reason for things to be awkward."

She stopped herself there. He was back because his mother was sick. Very sick, from what she was gathering, and she'd learned at any early age to follow a hunch.

Sean had made it clear when he left how he felt about this town and a career at her family's paper. That even her love for him wouldn't be enough to keep him here.

His mother had brought him back, sure, but she

wouldn't be the one to keep him here. Eventually, she'd get better, or... Annie closed her eyes; she couldn't think about it.

Either way, Sean would go back to the life he'd lived for more than half a decade. The one he wanted.

The one he'd chosen.

This week might be the last one they'd have. And his mother was sick. And she loved his mother. And she'd once loved him.

And unlike him, she had a heart. She wouldn't make this week worse than it needed to be for him.

Or for herself.

"Are you saying, Annie Baker, that we might be...friendly?" Sean's mouth twitched as all the sadness seemed to leave him.

He didn't say "friends" and Annie knew him well enough to know this was intentional. And even though being friends wasn't something she wanted, either, it hurt all the same that their relationship was reduced to what it was. That two people who once meant everything to each other could be nothing more than...friendly.

Her pulse quickened at the smile that tugged at his mouth and crinkled the corners of his eyes, but she didn't feed into it. She couldn't let her heart want things that it could never have.

"We're two grown adults," she said briskly. "We're thirty. There's no reason to let a childhood relationship get in the way of getting along for a few days. Of being professional."

"Professional." The smile faded from his face. "Is that all this is, then?"

Now it was Annie who didn't speak.

"And is that all we ever were? Childhood sweethearts?" He stared at her, his dark eyes stormy, searching.

"We were very young," she reminded him. Seventeen at their first kiss.

Twenty-four at their last.

But somehow, as her gaze fell to that mouth, and his full lips, now frowning, she could still remember exactly how it felt to be pulled into those strong arms, to feel the warmth of his mouth on hers, the taste of him.

"It has been a long time," he agreed, nodding along.

Even though it felt like yesterday.

With that, Annie hopped off the barstool. She glanced across the room and saw Travis talking with her cousins, occasionally glancing her way.

"Your brother's not with you tonight?" she asked Sean. See? She could do this. Converse. Ask normal questions. Pretend that her heart wasn't in her throat each time she looked at that face.

Sean gave her a knowing look, and once again she was reminded of the bond they shared. One that hadn't been broken, even now, no matter how badly she wished it might have been.

Sean and Drew had never been close, and it would seem that some things hadn't changed.

But others, like the two of them, had.

Much as she wished they hadn't.

Five

Sunday brunch at the Sweet Harmony Café was a tradition in the Baker household, dating back as far as Annie could remember to when her dad would take Caroline and her to enjoy fresh blueberry muffins while Valerie squirmed in her stroller. Their mother was always in and out of the kitchen or talking to patrons, but she always made time to sit and relax with the family for a few minutes, relying on her staff to handle the customers for a bit.

Today, the three sisters sat at a table near the window, as far from the kitchen as they could get, and today, Annie hoped that their mother stayed in the back, because this morning's topic of conversation was her.

"She even insisted on pink champagne," Annie stressed over her double-shot vanilla latte with extra foam and a sprinkle of cinnamon. She deserved a treat, and if today was gearing up to be anything like yesterday or the one before, she'd need all the help she could get.

"Yes, that's her new favorite *cocktail*, as she calls it." Molly cringed. "That and a cosmo."

"What happened to sauvignon blanc?" Annie cried. "Or rosé? It's pink!" Being a foodie, her mother knew how to pair wine, and whenever the sun shone in Seattle, which wasn't often enough in her opinion, and the weather was warm enough to sit outside and order fresh catch, Annie would order a crisp glass of rosé and think of summer evenings on the porch, her family gathered, and the conversation lively, the picnic table spread with overflowing lobster rolls, buttery corn on the cob, roasted vegetables fresh from the garden, and her mother at the helm, sipping a cold glass of wine from her cut crystal glasses that had been a wedding gift.

So much for the wineglasses. So much for what was in them.

"But Mom's always been a wine snob," Annie pressed, even though she knew it was pointless. Her sisters knew. And they also both seemed to sense that their mother was beyond their help.

"She's just having a bit of fun," Val said, letting her fork rest on her plate. The omelet she'd ordered was half-eaten, along with the pumpernickel toast, and Molly was picking at her pancakes. It seemed that they were all worried even if Valerie was trying not to show it. "It's harmless, really."

"*Harmless*? Do you think Dad feels that way?" Annie shook her head, grumbling to herself as she pushed away her avocado toast, not wanting to get too many crumbs on the table since her sisters would be getting up soon, and then she planned to take out her laptop and get some work done on her article. "I'm going to go see him after I leave here."

She'd texted her father, so he was expecting her. She'd insinuated that she wanted to interview him for her article, but she planned to drill him for much more personal information if possible.

"Good luck getting through to him," Val said with a sigh. The raise of her eyebrows revealed her doubts. "You know how he can be."

Annie nodded. She did. Their father was quiet, reserved, and deeply private. He liked to be the one asking the questions, not the one answering them. She'd be lucky to even get a few good quotes for her article about the paper's anniversary given how modest he was, but luckily he was also passionate, and she knew that when it came to his career, he wouldn't be able to hold back.

When it came to his marriage, she knew it wouldn't be quite so easy.

Molly took the last sip of her coffee and eyed the kitchen door. "I need to get back to work. Weekends are so busy, especially at this hour. But if you do talk to Dad, don't expect him to tell you how he feels. Anytime I've tried, he just tells me that he doesn't understand why she made him move out!"

"Do you think that's true?" Annie was bewildered. She'd always considered her father to be so intuitive.

Val seemed to consider it. "Maybe they didn't talk it out. Maybe Mom just made a decision and that was that."

"Poor Dad," Annie muttered.

"Well…" Molly hesitated. "You can't say that until you know both sides, can you?"

Annie knew that Molly was at least partly correct, if not

fully, but she couldn't get past the fact that their mother was not acting like the mother that she knew.

"He's the one who is living in the attic of the newspaper office," Annie replied.

"It's not a bad apartment..."

Annie shot Molly a warning look. "He still loves her," she concluded. "That's a good starting point."

"Yes, but does Mom still love him?" Valerie leaned forward and whispered, passing a meaningful look between Annie and Molly.

Annie looked at Molly, who had always been closest to their mother, while Annie had admittedly been a Daddy's girl.

Molly looked troubled until she shook her head sadly. "I don't know. She won't talk about him at all."

Val's lips curved when she glanced at Annie. "Well, you should know how to decode that."

"Me?" Annie's face burned when she took another sip of her latte. Sure, she hadn't wanted to discuss Sean after the breakup, and moving to Seattle had made that easier. So had time. Really, was it so unusual to not want to talk about the person who had broken your heart? To just want to move on?

But then she thought of the real reasons behind her resistance to talk about Sean. Talking about him meant thinking about him and that awful day when she'd felt like she'd been punched in the gut, her breath snatched straight from her lungs, her heart a heavy weight in her chest that didn't stop aching for months. It stirred up other memories, too—the good ones now made painful, like the time he'd won her a stuffed bear at the town carnival and then schlepped it around for the entire night so she could keep it, or how he'd silently reach over and hold her hand when they were watching a movie, or how she'd feel him looking at her from across the room at the *Herald*, and they'd share a small smile, and somehow, that made everything feel right in the world.

"I think there's a good chance that she still loves him," Annie said, then saw Val's eyes light up. "I'm not talking about me and Sean, Valerie. I'm talking about Mom and Dad. They've been married for thirty-five years. You don't just stop loving someone overnight."

Even though, she thought, she often wished that were possible.

"Well, don't expect to get anything out of Dad," Valerie said as she pushed back her chair. "But if you do, be sure to tell us."

"Like you were so sure to tell me?" Annie raised an eyebrow, but Val just grinned.

Molly collected their plates, insisting that it was her job and no trouble, and Annie leaned back in her chair, clutching her mug in both hands, watching as her mother now reappeared from the kitchen to greet some newcomers and guide them to an empty table. Her hair was in a perky ponytail today, but even Annie had to admit that her smile was bright.

Was it possible that she had stopped loving Annie's dad, that one morning she just woke up and decided that there would be no more family holidays, no more Christmases gathered around the tree that always took up half the living room because when they all trekked to the tree lot together, they couldn't resist the biggest one? No more Sunday brunches here at the café, with Dad reading over the morning edition, even though he knew every article by heart?

Annie felt the tears prickle the backs of her eyes, but they dried quickly when she saw Sean's mother walk through the door.

In the past, she might have used this opportunity to pick up her phone and make a quick call, or open her laptop, because Debbie Morrison was polite enough to take a hint, give a friendly wave, and be on her way.

But today, Annie smiled broadly and said, "Mrs. Morrison!"

Her table was open, her laptop was still in her tote bag, and there was an ache in her chest for lost time—not just with her own family, but with this woman, who almost had been.

"Annie!" Debbie's face lit up as she crossed the crowded room to where Annie sat, and it wasn't until she was standing in front of her that Annie saw how pale she looked, giving way to her worst fears.

Fighting back the growing sense of unease, Annie stood to hug Sean's mother, holding on a little longer than she had in the past.

Debbie's smile was wan when they pulled apart. "You've heard the news, then."

Annie blinked, trying to think of the right thing to say and falling very short. "Only that you haven't been well. And...that Sean came back to town."

Debbie sighed, and Annie motioned for her to sit. But as soon as she was seated, her expression seemed to brighten.

"Having Sean back has been so wonderful," she said, stressing every word. Then, with a glimmer in her soft brown eyes, she glanced at Annie. "You've seen him, then?"

Oh, dear. The last thing that Annie wanted was to give the woman false hope. She knew that Debbie pined for grandkids, now probably more than ever, and it wasn't like her oldest son was going to be assisting in that endeavor anytime soon. Few women on the Cape would find Drew attractive, and it had nothing to do with his looks, which were nearly—but not quite—as handsome as Sean's.

Drew was the spitting image of his father, from his career path to his temperament, which was brash, ruthless, and self-serving. Everyone in Harmony Cove marveled over how Sean's parents had ever come to be, how Debbie brought out the softer side of Bill, and how Sean took after his mother. Drew would be so lucky to ever find a woman who was half as kind and generous as his mother, and Annie suspected that he never would and that sadly, his mother knew it.

"I saw him at the paper," Annie said, tipping her head in question. Perhaps Debbie could explain how this had come to be, her illness aside. Surely Sean couldn't truly be content at the *Herald*, not after traveling the globe, covering the biggest news events for the last six years?

"Must have been quite a surprise" was all she said.

Annie chuckled, even though it wasn't exactly funny. "For both of us, I think."

Debbie opened her mouth to say something and then closed it again. Annie waited patiently. She'd learned from her aunt Marcy that if you sat quietly and gave someone a chance to open up, they often would.

"I'm sure that it meant a lot to Sean to see you again," Debbie said carefully.

Annie tried to keep her expression from betraying the war of emotions that was raging inside her, making her pulse quicken and her hands shake a little. She didn't trust herself to speak, for fear of looking desperate and asking Sean's mother what she knew.

To seem like she still cared.

"Leaving this town wasn't easy for him," Debbie added.

But he'd done it, anyway.

Annie felt her anger stir, but she wasn't about to start an argument with this woman. Not when she'd always been kind to her. Not when she was sick. And not when the only thing she could be accused of was seeing the good in her son.

It was certainly more than Sean's father could ever do.

"You know he loved you," Debbie pressed.

Loved. Past tense.

Had Sean moved on with someone else? His mother would know. She'd probably even tell Annie if she asked.

"Yep," Annie said, and even that one-syllable word felt shaky. "I also know how much he loves his career."

Shoot. It was the wrong thing to say. She saw the shadow pass over Debbie's face, the knowledge that she had taken her son away from the career he'd given up everything—and everything else—for.

"But more than anything, he loves you," Annie said softly. She reached out and took the other woman's hand, giving it a tight squeeze.

Sean's mother held on to Annie as her eyes brimmed with tears before she quickly recovered herself. After a shaky sigh, she leaned into the table and said, "Sean may not be happy for the reasons he returned to town, but something tells me that he's happy to be home. Especially now that you're back."

"Oh…" Annie didn't want Debbie to get any notions that there was a chance at her reuniting with Sean. Not after all these years. Not when she didn't even live in Harmony Cove anymore. "I'm leaving a week from today," she said gently.

"Sometimes, for better or worse, we get called home." Debbie gave her a slow smile. "And if we're lucky, we stop and listen."

With that, she stood, pushing her chair back with a trembling hand and waving off Annie's efforts to help her.

"I'm not dining in today. I just popped in for one of your mother's muffins. It's too nice of a day to sit inside. I thought I'd walk down to the harbor and watch the boats for a bit." She smiled. "We'll see each other again, I hope."

"Of course!" Annie said, hearing the alarm rise in her voice, hoping that Debbie hadn't heard it, too.

But as she sat back down and stared out the window, watching a few minutes later as Debbie Morrison left the building and moved slowly down the street, she wasn't so sure that would be true. Everything had changed since her last visit.

How much more would change before her next?

A short while later, and only after Annie had insisted to her mother at least half a dozen times that it meant nothing to her that Sean was back in town and that she'd simply been neighborly to chat with his mother, Annie sat in her father's office, a room as familiar to her as any room in her childhood home, with its smell of old wood, lemon furniture polish, and strong coffee. She had a page full of notes to include in her article, and her father seemed happy to discuss the history of the *Herald* all day, and not just because of his obvious love for it.

"Why didn't you tell me that you were writing an article about the paper?" he asked, seeming both pleased and perplexed.

Annie gave a watery smile. Her big announcement felt trivial in comparison with the news of her parents' split. "I wanted it to be a surprise."

"Ah. Well, it is." He grinned. "And it's something different from your usual column."

Leave it to her father to home in on that. Seeing no way around explaining the departure, Annie braced herself. "It is. There's an opportunity for a promotion. This article might be my chance to stand out and be recognized."

She watched her father closely as this news sunk in. His shoulders sank a little, he sat back in his chair, and his features softened when he pulled off his reading glasses. "Oh, honey. I'm *so proud* of you."

"I haven't gotten the promotion yet, Dad," she warned him.

And she wasn't even sure she wanted it.

He brushed a hand through the air, dismissing her

concern, and Annie felt a wave of dread as she went back to her notes.

If she focused on the paper and her father's legacy, maybe she could forget why she was writing this article.

"Dad—" she started, but his eyes flashed on hers.

"You know that Sean is writing an article on the paper's anniversary, too," her father said, giving his bushy eyebrows a little wiggle.

Annie sucked in a sigh. "I'm not here to discuss my relationship with Sean." Or lack thereof, was more like it. "I'm here to talk about the paper. For my article. And—"

"And your promotion! I know you'll get it, sweetheart, and I know that you've earned it. You took everything that you learned here and ran with it. Why, I wouldn't be surprised if you were running that paper in Seattle one day."

Annie gave a nervous laugh.

"People ask about you all the time, and I always tell them that you're a city girl now, working in a big high-rise, with a byline in a well-known paper. Maybe it's bragging, but can a father stop himself from being proud of his daughter?"

There was that word again. *Proud*.

Would he still be proud if she didn't get the promotion? If her move to Seattle was for nothing?

He'd encouraged her to go when he saw how much it was hurting her to stay in Harmony Cove without Sean, but instead of the job being a temporary solution, it had become a permanent change and one she had never been able to fully embrace. And maybe that was because instead of running to a life she wanted, she was running from the one she'd loved.

"You've made a name for yourself, too, Dad," Annie

insisted. "It's not about the size of the town. Or the readership."

Her father shook his head as he leaned back in his wooden banker's chair. "Don't get me wrong, I love this paper, this was where I only ever wanted to be, and knowing it was all my own made it feel important. But what you're doing is..."

Uninspiring. Unrewarding. Deeply lonely. To name a few.

"I save all your articles, you know. I have a digital subscription so I can print them out."

"They're just about parties and events—"

"Nonsense! You're writing about your new city. That's not much different than what we do here."

Except that it was because Harmony Cove was a community, where everyone knew each other and cared, too. Here, the articles about the town were relevant to everyday life. In Seattle, she was writing about people she'd never met, and anyone who turned to her article would find themselves reading about strangers.

"You're taking everything I taught you to a new level." Her father's grin stretched his cheeks and made his eyes shine.

Yep. All the way across the country. Away from everything and everyone she loved most. It was supposed to be what she needed. It was supposed to be her second chance.

It was supposed to make her father proud.

At least she'd checked one box.

Annie felt a lump rise in her throat. "Well, you gave me wings, Dad. Encouraging me to go."

"Encouraging you to live to your fullest potential! And you have, honey. And I am so, so, so proud of you."

Annie pulled in a shaky breath and looked back at her notes, telling herself that she would make him proud, because she didn't feel proud. Not yet. Not of her current job. Not of how infrequently she got back to town. Not when she knew that her entire family was falling apart in her absence.

She shouldn't have stayed away just because it was easier than being here and feeling everything that she missed.

She never should have gone away in the first place. Because ever since she did, coming home no longer felt like an option.

"Dad," she began again, but when she saw the smile start to slip from his face, she stopped herself. Her sisters were right. Their father didn't want to talk about his marital problems, at least not with them. And he'd trained her firsthand to know when to push someone for information and when to stop.

She would stop. For today.

"I guess I just have a few more questions," she said. Then, giving him a pointed look, added, "For now."

He tented his fingers and leaned back in his chair. "Ask me anything. The paper is my favorite topic. Other than you girls, of course."

"And why is that?" she asked. "Why do you love the paper so much? Is it the news? The process?"

"It's the family aspect," her father said simply.

Annie jotted this down even as her heartstrings pulled tight. Her father was a family man, but now half of his daughters lived far away and rarely—or never in Caroline's case—visited. And his marriage seemed to be all but over.

"And the community," he added. "Running this paper has allowed me to carry on not just the family name but something that has mattered to the town of Harmony Cove for longer than I've been alive. Knowing that I'm handing off something that will outlive me—"

"Wait." Annie stared at her father across the desk, her heart quickening. "What do you mean, *handing off the paper*?"

Mitch paused before giving her an apologetic smile. "I can't run the paper forever, sweetheart."

Couldn't he? Annie hadn't ever considered her father anywhere but behind this desk. He didn't just work here, he lived here. (Well, no need to dwell on that at the moment.)

This paper was like a fifth child to him. Like a second love, she thought as her mind went to her mother and what she'd said.

This paper was a part of their family. A legacy.

"But you're not that old—" She quickly did the math. He was only sixty-two! She had a coworker her age back in Seattle who was dating a man who was fifty-nine! Slightly scandalous, yes, but still.

"It has nothing to do with age," her father replied mildly. "I've always known that when the time came, I'd know. And these past few months, I've thought about it more and more."

"But..." Annie was at a loss for words. There was too much change. Too much loss. She couldn't think of this paper without picturing her father, remembering all the days he'd let her tag along, how even when he was at home, he was talking about another story he might want to feature and bring to the community. The girls used to love to share all their updates from school, feeling like they'd won a special prize if their news was newspaper-worthy.

Annie usually won.

"I guess I just never saw you retiring," Annie finally admitted. She looked around the room with its tall, wide windows looking down on to Water Street. Would Marcy move in, as the rightful heir? Annie couldn't imagine what would happen to the paper if she did.

"You've got a big promotion on the line," he said as if she needed the reminder. "And I'm going to do everything I can to support that. So here's the scoop: my last day at the paper will be on the anniversary. It's my swan song. My final edition. It just feels right."

More like it felt so wrong.

"You're the first person I've told," Mitch said, looking at her as if he expected her to be happy for him.

Annie stared at her father, officially silenced. There was so much she wanted to say and couldn't.

Her father's smile was gentle. "I've done everything I wanted to with this paper, including raising a talented journalist who has taken our family business and grown it far beyond the reaches of the *Herald*'s circulation."

She'd made her father proud. He was retiring a happy man, satisfied with what he'd accomplished—and with what *she'd* accomplished.

Only she didn't feel like she'd accomplished anything at

all other than running away from everyone she loved the most.

Sean was on his third cup of coffee and he'd already finished his article that was due today—the article on the Reynolds's hotel development that had people divided over the land use. Personally, he thought it was a good idea, one that would further bolster tourism and support the local economy, maybe even through the cold winter months when a lot of small businesses were known to struggle. But he was a reporter, and this wasn't an opinion piece, so he kept his feelings out of it.

It wouldn't be so easy to do with the anniversary article, and not just because Annie was collaborating with him. This paper meant a lot to him. But not as much as Mitch did.

Or Annie.

He stood and stretched his legs, knowing that his work was done for the day, and he should probably go home. Instead, he walked toward the cramped office kitchen for a refill, nearly colliding with Annie as she stepped out of Mitch's office.

"Hello," he said, starting to smile at her until he saw that her eyes were rimmed with red, and a brighter blue than usual, a sure sign that she'd been crying, or was about to start. Old instincts kicked in as he felt his expression slip and his chest tighten. "Is everything okay?"

She hesitated, and he understood. They weren't close

anymore, and the days of telling each other everything had ended when he broke up with her.

When he broke her trust.

"It's fine," she said, giving a little sniff. "I'm surprised to see you here on a Sunday morning."

He shrugged. "You know better than anyone that the paper never sleeps."

"I also know that you don't have to come into the office to file an article," she said with a look of interest.

What could he say? He'd rather be here than at home, where he was either constantly reminded of his mother's failing health or his father's low opinion of him. It was nothing new, the part about his father, of course, but it never got easier, even after years away—and that time that he'd lost with his mother—and Annie, well, that was something he could never forgive his father for.

Or himself.

"I ran into your mother this morning," Annie said. "At the café."

Sean's smile slipped. His mother still insisted on her daily walks, even if it was just to go to the café for a cup of tea. He knew it meant a lot to her to be around people she'd known all her life, to feel like she was part of the living and not the...

He stopped himself right there. No sense in thinking about that.

"My mom has always loved Sweet Harmony," he said, dodging the real issue. He felt it as much as Annie did, this reluctance to open up, but not because he couldn't trust her, because he didn't feel it was fair. She wasn't his girlfriend anymore. She wasn't even a friend. He'd lost that right to share his innermost thoughts and fears with her the day that he'd boarded that ferry and never looked back.

No matter how many times he'd wanted to.

"It's the one thing in my family that hasn't changed," Annie muttered.

Sean narrowed his eyes, knowing that there was more to that comment than she was letting on. No doubt she wasn't taking the news of her parents' separation well.

"Well, the paper's still the same," Sean said as he filled his mug with coffee.

"For now," Annie said as a shadow crossed her face.

Now Sean frowned at her, deciding it was time to come out with it. "Is there something going on?"

"No," Annie said quickly. "I just... Sometimes it's hard not to wish that everything could just stay the same, the way it used to be, back when I was younger, when everything about this town felt certain, you know?"

Did he ever. Sean would do anything to turn back time, to be the younger version of himself with his entire future ahead of him and the girl he loved wanting to share it. But he nodded instead, holding himself back from telling her just how much he understood. It wouldn't change the facts. And the fact was that he'd left this town and her, and the action mattered more than the reason behind it.

"I thought maybe we could work on the article tomorrow," he suggested. "I'd love to see some old photos of your dad."

"Photos." The idea seemed to dawn on Annie for the first time. "They were always in shoeboxes, in the den. I think they're still there. I mean...I hope so."

Meaning that she was hoping that Sharon Baker hadn't pitched them along with her husband.

Sean hoped so, too.

"I'll swing by tomorrow if that works for you?" Sean tried to keep the hope out of his voice. This was professional, not personal. But it was still an excuse to spend time together.

"Stop by after lunch," Annie said. "Molly and my mother will both be at the café until late afternoon."

In other words, they'd be alone, just the two of them.

He was about to make a joke about that, to feel her out, or add some levity to this tension that pulsed between them, but Annie's worried expression made him reconsider.

He couldn't risk having Annie change her mind about letting him into her house—or a small corner of her life.

Not when he'd never once wavered about how he felt about her in all these years.

Six

Sean showed up at the house at one o'clock sharp, taking the back door like he always did, and Annie supposed that she was grateful for that; if he'd knocked on the front door, it would have felt too formal, confirming that they were strangers now, instead of reminding her that they shared a past, and one that he remembered.

Even if it was all that bound them now.

Annie was in the kitchen when she heard the tires of his car crunch over the gravel, and she'd had to take three deep breaths to steady herself before he appeared at the screen door, wearing khaki pants and a button-down shirt rolled at the sleeves, looking so grown-up and professional that she couldn't help but remind herself that they weren't twenty-two-year-old college graduates anymore.

And she wasn't his girl anymore, either.

"I figured that my days of just letting myself in were over," Sean said sheepishly when Annie pushed open the door to let him step inside.

It was a warm spring day, but the sky was overcast, threatening rain, which was just as well, considering that Annie planned to spend the day inside, going through the old photo boxes she'd dug out of the closet in the den and drafting her article.

Besides, it fit her mood. Since learning that her father planned to retire, she could barely think of anything else, and it had taken everything in her not to tell her mother and see if that got a reaction out of her. But her mother had stayed late at the café last night waiting on a supplier, and she and Molly had both rolled in after Annie was in bed, by then too tired, and, frankly, emotionally drained, to confront them. She'd thought about it again this morning, while they had a family breakfast of eggs and toast, which Annie made to give her mother a much-needed break, but they were getting along so well, and her mother seemed so happy, that again, Annie kept the information to herself.

But now, it felt like it was about to burst from her. Her father. Leaving the family paper. On the one-hundredth anniversary.

This would be his last week running the paper.

It didn't seem possible.

It didn't make sense.

But then, what did anymore?

"I found some boxes of old photos," Annie said, dodging Sean's comment, because the last thing she wanted was to get into another conversation about their past when she wanted to focus on the paper's history instead. It was already Monday, meaning she had less than a week to do her father's legacy justice.

To make him proud.

"Great." Sean looked eagerly toward the coffee table in the adjacent living room, where Annie had set out everything she'd found, after her mother had left for the café, of course. Given her mother's recent behavior, Annie wasn't sure what would happen to the photos and memorabilia of happier times if they weren't tucked away for safe keeping.

A roll of thunder seemed to shake the house, and a moment later, rain began with the speed and force of a waterfall.

"Looks like I got here just in time," Sean remarked. Then, looking at her T-shirt, which was dampened by the gust of wind that had blown rain through the screen door, he said, "I could start a fire if you'd like. It would warm things up while we work."

Annie nodded. A fire would be nice, and most of her happiest memories in this living room were the ones of the family gathered around the hearth, her parents sharing the love seat, while the four Baker girls curled up on the long sofa, dangling their legs over the armchair, or spread out on the large wool area rug, reading books, or playing board games on the wooden coffee table where the boxes and albums of their family history now sat.

She'd thought those days would last forever. Even after she and Caroline left town, Annie had assumed that somehow that picture-perfect moment would still repeat itself at the holidays or other visits, that the family would even grow over the years as her sisters married and had children.

Instead, their family was shrinking. Caroline would

likely never return once she learned about Hillary marrying Tim. Val and Molly hadn't dated in years, at least not seriously. And their father hadn't been back in this house since September—and it seemed that their mother had no intentions of letting him back in anytime soon. If ever again.

While Sean started the fire, Annie dropped to the faded rug and pulled a stack of photos from the box closest to her. They were old and faded, a few torn at the edges.

She smiled as she sorted through the pile that appeared to be in no order, not that she was surprised. Her mother was many things but organized was not one of them. She had her systems, but to outsiders, they would classify her kitchen at the café and even this house to be a bit of a ramshackle.

"Is that you?" Sean asked as he came to sit beside her, the fire now blazing in the hearth.

Annie was holding a picture of her family, back when they were still all so young, taken outside the ice cream shop in town. She must have been about four, but it was her mother that she couldn't stop staring at, with her then blond hair long and wavy, falling halfway down her back. She was tanned, sun-kissed at the shoulders in her cotton dress, baby Molly on her hip, and her handsome young husband at her side. Annie and her sisters were lined up in a row on a wooden bench, each holding ice cream cones. Valerie was actively licking hers, Caroline was dutifully grinning at the camera, and Annie was frowning down at her ice cream, as if afraid it would melt before the picture was taken.

"You look so worried in this photo," Sean observed with an amused glance in her direction.

Annie looked more closely at her younger self, feeling a

wave of nostalgia for time gone by, wishing that she could have clung to that moment a little longer, or at least not taken it for granted.

If only a melting ice cream cone were her biggest problem now. Did the people in this photo know that twenty-some years later that smiling wife would kick her husband out of their family home on their wedding anniversary and their oldest daughter's birthday to boot? Did the earnest little girl with blond hair like her mother know that her fiancé would be a no-show on her wedding day and then propose to her best friend and cousin a few years later?

Nope. They hadn't a clue. Only Val seemed to have managed to get it right so far. She just trucked through life. No matter what hit her, she kept on going; nothing stopped her from enjoying that ice cream.

"Here's one from high school," Sean said, pulling another from the pile.

"Let me see that." Annie snatched it from him, hoping it wasn't one from her mortifying headgear years.

But what she saw was almost worse. It was from the summer before their senior year, she could tell because she'd begged her mother for highlights that year and had finally worn her down. Annie was on the beach with Caroline, Hillary, Tim, and a few of the other kids they used to hang out with back then. They were sitting on old blankets, and the sky was swirled with cotton candy colors as evening set in.

She was wearing Sean's sweatshirt. He had his arm around her.

Her head rested casually against his shoulder.

"We look so happy," he said quietly.

She was thinking the same thing.

Happier than even she could remember being. The kind of happiness that you thought would last forever, that you never doubted, and simply enjoyed.

"This must be from the summer we started dating," Sean went on.

Annie pinched her lips even as her heart began to pound. She didn't like thinking about those days when the future seemed bright and full of endless possibilities. When Sean was a part of her life and not just a moment from her past.

She cleared her throat and pulled up another box. "Well, we should probably go back further if we're going to find any of my dad when *he* was young."

The next box proved to be a better starting point. She flipped through photos of Aunt Marcy, so youthful with her now-gray hair then dark, falling at her shoulders in soft waves. She wore glasses even when she was younger, but her face was full, her smile bright, and her eyes, as always, inquisitive.

"I wonder why Marcy never got married," Sean mused as warmth filled the room and the sound of crackling logs filled the silence.

"She wanted to," Annie said, thinking of the long sighs Marcy would give here and there when she wrote about another couple getting engaged or married. How Annie's father was always sure to include his sister for holidays, sensing that she was lonely.

Now Marcy was in her late-fifties, and the realization

that her aunt never had the opportunity to have a family made Annie's heart ache.

"There was someone once," Annie said, vaguely remembering talk of Marcy having a beau in her younger days. "But love doesn't always last."

She couldn't look at Sean, afraid of what she might feel or say if she did.

"More like it doesn't always work out," Sean said quietly. "True love doesn't ever really end."

Annie glanced at Sean as he moved over to her, shifting his body away from the fireplace so that he could see the photo she was holding, his body so close that she could smell the aftershave he'd always used, that woodsy sent that made her feel like she was right where she needed to be.

Did true love really last? She wanted to believe it, for her parents' sake if not for her own, because she'd long ago given up thinking that Sean loved her.

Or ever really had.

She scooted over to the right, needing space from the man she once only ever wanted to have close. She passed him the photo, then moved on to another, this one of Marcy and her father standing outside the building of the paper, both smiling. She set it aside as a keeper. Even if she didn't use it in her article, she'd make a copy and frame it for both her father and aunt.

"She was pretty back then," Sean said, studying the photo in his hand. "But then, she's related to you, so I shouldn't be surprised."

Annie refused to feed into the flattery. So he still found

her pretty. Just like she still found him handsome. Some things didn't change, even if she wished they would.

"You don't get to say things like that anymore." Boundaries were needed if they were going to get through the week, and she didn't need anything distracting her from this article, especially when now, knowing that it was the last one she'd write while her father still owned the paper, the pressure had doubled.

It was no longer just about a small-town paper thriving in a digital era, it was about the impact her father had on Harmony Cove.

And on her.

"Can I help it if I think you're the most beautiful woman I've ever known?" Sean replied, his expression frank.

Annie huffed out a sigh. "If you're trying to get on my good side, there's no need. You're already here. I've let you in. We're collaborating. What more do you want?"

"A lot more," Sean said, his attention solely on her now. His dark eyes locked with hers, searching for something that she didn't think she could give him. "I don't want things to be like this between us."

"Like what?" Annie asked, hoping that he wasn't going to ask for her forgiveness, because she didn't think she could offer it, and she felt too tired from poor sleep the past three nights to argue with him.

"Distant," he said. "Cold."

"We're just two people working on an article together," she told him with a sigh, even though she knew that it was more than that. That no matter how much she wished that

Sean didn't still matter, she still cared what he said or did, and she still felt a pull when she was close to him.

She inched away farther, needing space, but wanting just the opposite.

Wanting, perhaps, to go back in time. For him to have never boarded that ferry.

For him to have chosen her.

"But we were once a lot more than that, Annie," he said, still staring at her.

Her mouth went dry as her heart started to pound, and she wanted to tear her eyes away from his but found that she couldn't.

"If I was so important to you, then why'd you go?" Annie countered, mad at herself for even engaging in this. It was ancient history!

But oh, when she looked into those deep brown eyes, it felt like yesterday.

"Does it matter?" he asked.

She studied his face for a moment, knowing that it probably didn't, because the facts were the facts and couldn't be changed. Whatever the reasons, he'd made his choice.

But why would anyone choose to leave the person they claimed to love?

"It does," she said, wishing so much that it didn't.

Sean paused for a long moment and then sat back against the couch. "I guess I felt like I had something to prove. To my father."

Annie shook her head. She knew how his father was, how he'd always favored Sean's brother, seeing him as his likeness, both in appearance and in everything else. She knew that Sean had disappointed him when he didn't go into law, and she knew that it bothered Sean that his brother would take over the family firm one day. "But you made the choice not to follow in his footsteps."

"And he never stopped punishing me for it," Sean ground out. He pulled in a long breath, steadying his temper, which always flared when his father was mentioned. Even now, the hurt was still there.

It went to show that as much as things had changed recently, some things stayed the same.

"You know what he thought of my journalism degree," Sean said. "I thought that if I got a graduate degree, that would help. It didn't." His jaw tensed. "I'm not sure anything would make him see me as worthy."

Annie saw the hurt in his eyes and felt a familiar wave of protectiveness for him. "Who couldn't be proud of you? You were on the front line, you were telling the stories that people needed to hear, giving a voice to victims, giving them a chance to be seen."

Darn. She'd just sort of admitted that she'd followed his career over the years, but instead of looking amused or even flattered by this, Sean seemed defeated.

"I know. And I told myself the same thing every day. And you know, for a while, my father was proud." He looked at her darkly. "But I wasn't."

Silence fell over the room as Annie considered his words, listening to the logs crackling in the fireplace. He'd left everything he'd loved—even, supposedly, her—to chase a career, to do important things, but he didn't feel good about it.

And as much as she hated to admit it, she understood that feeling. More than he knew.

"Look, I understand why you left," Annie said, because she did, even if she hadn't back then. She was too young, and too in love. She thought that love trumped all. That nothing could touch it. Or ruin it.

She'd thought that it would last forever.

Now her eyes drifted from the only man she'd ever loved to the empty spot on the mantel where her parents' wedding photo used to sit in a silver-plated frame.

Who was she kidding? Nothing lasted forever.

"So," Annie said, curling her long legs under her as she leaned into the coffee table. "How does your father feel about you working at the *Harmony Herald*?"

"He understands the reasons I'm here," Sean said, his gut tightening the way it did every time he thought about his mother. It wasn't like he could talk about it with his father or brother—they both used work as their excuse to hide from the reality of what was happening at home. But then, the law firm had always been his father's top priority, even now.

Sean's mother assured him that it was fine, that she was happy that his father had another passion, and that it would help him once she was gone. And that was when the conversation always ended. When he wanted to put his hands over his ears, but didn't. When instead, he'd find a reason to leave the room. When he'd reduce himself to his father's ways.

When he was finally, at long last, his father's son.

Annie's eyes were filled with so much sympathy that Sean had to look away. It was easier to think about something, anything other than what hurt the most.

What mattered the most.

It's what he'd done all these years, burying himself in a story, hopping on a plane and chasing the action, telling himself that he was where he needed to be even though none of it felt right.

"And your job in DC?" Annie was looking at him expectantly, and Sean knew that he couldn't lie.

"They're holding it for me," he said, seeing a shadow pass through her eyes.

"So you're only here temporarily." Annie nodded, then, perhaps seeing the anguish in his face, she added, quickly, "I mean, when your mother gets better..."

His mother wasn't going to get better, but he couldn't think about that much less say it. And he couldn't bring himself to say that his job at the *Herald* or his time here in town was short-term, either, even if that's exactly what his father thought it was. It was the only reason he wasn't giving him grief for writing stories about things like the upcoming high school graduation events or the new hotel development.

"What about you?" he asked, needing to get off the topic of his career choices—or lack thereof. "You don't have any plans to return to Harmony Cove anytime soon?"

"Oh, well, I have a job in Seattle," Annie said, shifting a little as she started sorting through the box again.

Sean watched her, sensing that she didn't want to talk about her life in Seattle—maybe because it didn't include him, never had, and never would. Or maybe because, like him, she'd learned that bigger cities and opportunities weren't always better.

"Your father can't stop talking about your big promotion," Sean said, but instead of bringing the expected smile to Annie's face, he watched her flinch.

"It's not a done deal."

Sean nodded. "But I don't see why you wouldn't get it. You're a great reporter, and you have a strong work ethic. And you learned from the best."

They both had.

Annie riffled through the box of photos. "I just want to make my father proud, you know?"

Sean looked at her in surprise. "I can't remember a time when your father wasn't proud of you, Annie."

Now she looked at him, guilt clouding her expression. "I don't mean to be insensitive. I know that my dad has always been supportive. He helped get me the job in Seattle, and...I just want to make sure he knows he was right to believe in me. That I didn't waste the opportunity."

"I don't think Mitch will be any less proud of you if you don't get the promotion," Sean said, knowing it was true, and wishing that the same could be said for his father, who measured love with merit, whose affection had to be earned —the hard way.

Annie nodded, but he could tell that she was still troubled when she went back to her task, flipping through photos, stopping after every few for a longer look. Her mouth curved as she pulled one closer. "I forgot all about this."

Curious, Sean leaned in, catching a hint of the scent of her coconut shampoo when he did. He smiled at the memory it turned up, awakening a pull inside him that he struggled to put in check. Fighting against the attraction, he focused on the image in her hand. It was a photo of Mitch, taken when he was much younger, back when he was about twenty pounds thinner and still had a full head of thick brown hair. He was sitting at a table at the Sweet Harmony Café, frowning in concentration over a legal pad, his pen poised over the page.

"My mother must have taken this," Annie said softly. "He used to work there sometimes, back when she first opened the café. He said it inspired him, that he got all his best ideas there. He said that there was always a story to tell from that place because half the town came through the door on any given day."

Sean saw her eyes mist for a moment.

"May I?" Sean took the photo before it got lost in the disorganized shuffle. He studied it before carefully setting it beside the one of Mitch and Marcy. "I think this one's worth holding on to. The best memories are, even if that's all they are."

Her eyes locked his for a moment, and he thought he saw understanding pass through them. He knew that she might never forgive him, but he hoped that she'd at least believe him when he said that he hadn't stopped loving her that day.

That maybe he never had.

"I'm sorry about your parents," Sean said softly. No one could have been more surprised than him to learn that the Bakers had broken up—well, other than Annie.

And maybe Mitch. The man had seemed mildly embarrassed to share his living situation with Sean that first day back on the job when he'd noticed Mitch open the back door to the top floor after they'd put the edition to bed. He'd laughed it off and made it sound like a little tiff, but months had gone by and nothing had changed, and Sean knew better than to say anything. Everyone did.

Even Marcy.

"It's not just that." Annie seemed to hesitate. "Did you see my father this morning at the office? Did he...mention anything?"

Sean replayed the brief conversation he'd had with Mitch at the coffee machine. The man had seemed more than pleased that Sean and Annie were collaborating on the story, not that Sean would tell Annie that. Instead, he said, "He knows that we're teaming up on this story, if that's what you mean."

"He didn't give you any...scoop, then?" Annie peered at him, and Sean momentarily got lost in the depth of her eyes, the sprinkle of freckles on her nose from childhood days spent out in the sun, and the pull in his chest that made him want to reach out and touch her. And this time, to never let her go.

"Scoop?" Sean frowned and then jabbed Annie with a finger. "Hey, we promised to share information. Don't tell me you're keeping something from me."

But Annie didn't reply. She didn't even tell him not to touch her.

Something must be very wrong.

"What's going on, Annie?" he asked, growing worried.

He couldn't help it; the news of his mother had come as a blow, and the fear of losing someone else he loved was all too real.

"I'm sure it's something you'll find out soon enough. Maybe even today." She lowered her eyes, then swallowed slowly before looking at him again. "My dad's retiring. The anniversary will be his last day at the paper."

Sean saw the tears fill Annie's eyes and had to resist the urge to put an arm around her, to pull her close, kiss her hair, her cheeks. Her lips.

"I didn't know," he said, feeling genuinely shocked at the news. Heck, he felt like he could break down and cry along with Annie, if he were the crying type, that was. Instead, he drew a breath and let the news soak in, trying to make sense of it and to imagine the paper without Mitch Baker.

It would be a loss. For him. For the town.

"I assume he hasn't told *anyone*," Sean said, thinking out loud. "This isn't the kind of news that Marcy could hold in for long."

Annie sputtered on a laugh as tears fell from her eyes. She wiped them away quickly, but more continued to fall.

"I don't know why I'm crying like this," she admitted. "My dad is in his sixties. He has the right to retire. He's certainly earned it."

"No one works harder than your father," Sean agreed. But unlike his own father, who clocked long hours at the firm, Mitch Baker had his priorities straight. He loved his work because he loved the community, and he loved the people of this town, most importantly his family. The man was so invested in every word that went into the paper. It was important to him that each edition wasn't just factually correct, but fulfilling, that the readers wouldn't be let down, and that they were getting the news that mattered—maybe not to people like Sean's father, but to those who saw Harmony Cove as more than just a pretty place to live.

The thought of him no longer being there every day, skimming over the columns, rolling his eyes at the Harmony Happenings section, and then grinning ear to ear when everything finally went to print, filled Sean with a sense of sadness that he knew only Annie could share as deeply as he did.

"Please don't tell him that I told you," Annie begged. "He might assume I did, since we're sharing resources for the article, but—"

"I won't say a word," Sean assured her quickly, meaning it. She'd opened up to him, and trusted him with this, and as glad as he was that she felt she could share this news with him, he wished she hadn't because he didn't want it to be true. "He'll have to tell everyone this week, anyway." He did a quick calculation, finding it incredulous. "Six more days."

"Six," Annie echoed. "Not years or months or even weeks. But days."

Another countdown, Sean thought. Another timebomb, ticking away, stealing someone he'd loved.

"Why don't we plan something for him, for this weekend?" he suggested, desperate to focus on something he could control.

"You mean like a retirement party?" Annie looked doubtful. "I don't know how we can do that without revealing his plans."

"So, we'll tell them it's a party for the hundredth anniversary of the paper," Sean suggested, the idea growing on him. "We can do it Saturday night after his last edition."

They both grew quiet as the reality of that implication set in.

"By then, everyone will know. We can give him a special honor," Sean went on. He tried to cajole Annie, who didn't seem to share his enthusiasm. "We can celebrate finishing our articles, too."

Annie wasn't smiling with him, but the tears had at least stopped falling. "I think we owe him that much. At least, I do."

"I do, too," Sean said firmly, holding her gaze and hoping that she believed him.

He looked back at the photo of a younger Mitch Baker, working hard in his new wife's café, and he felt homesick even though he was home right here in Harmony Cove.

He knew that feeling, of being inspired, of doing your best work, surrounded by your favorite people. It was how Sean had felt every day since being back at the *Herald*, mentored by a man who didn't just care about putting out the news, but about the people who were reading it.

He was a good man. The kind of man that Sean wanted to be—but wasn't. And maybe, if his father had his way, never would be.

Seven

The way Annie saw it, an emergency meeting of the sisters was in order. They agreed on Tuesday night when their mother had her monthly book club at the Book Nook, the quaint store owned by Kathy's daughter Emily. Location didn't matter to Annie; she wasn't going to eat. But when Val suggested the Lighthouse Grill, Annie felt her spirits lift. One of the oldest establishments around, it was the only oceanfront restaurant in all of Harmony Cove, since the center of town had been built on the bayside.

"I almost feel like a traitor ordering their chowder," she told her sisters when they were seated at a table on the patio with a view of the water. The sun had already set, but the colors still clung to the sky, casting a warm pink glow over the beach and reflecting off the gentle ocean waves.

"They're famous for it here!" Molly reassured her. "It would be wrong not to order it."

"You're right," Annie said, decision made. Even under the heat lamp, she shivered in her cashmere cardigan. Soup was exactly what she needed right now. Warm. Comforting. Familiar.

Everything that home usually was, but certainly no longer felt like.

"So, any more Sean sightings?" Val asked once their glasses of wine were delivered and their orders taken. "According to Marcy's column today, the two of you were seen 'canoodling' in the office the other day."

"Canoodling?" Annie snorted into her sauvignon blanc and then took a long sip. Marcy certainly loved to exaggerate.

"She went on to say that in a burst of passion, Sean tugged you into his office and then promptly closed the door," Valerie continued, unable to hide her amusement. "I clipped the article and have it in my handbag if you'd like to see it for yourself."

"Give that to me!" Annie snatched it from her sister's hand once Valerie had fished it from her tote.

She scanned the column, glossing over the rumors of the mayor not going up for reelection, the shenanigans that had taken place in the women's first tennis match of the season, where, suspiciously, partners had been swapped in the off-season for reasons yet to be revealed (or uncovered), and slowed down when she reached the last paragraph, which described two unnamed former lovebirds who had both found their way back to the nest.

"You have got to be kidding me," Annie groaned. The article went on to say that the pair remained behind closed doors for long enough to suggest that their business wasn't just private but personal.

"What did she think we were doing in there?" Annie

asked, tucking the article into her bag, despite Val trying to reach for it.

"Sounds to me like she thought you two were enjoying yourself in more than a professional manner," Val replied, sharing a laugh with Molly.

"More like hiding from her," Annie said with a shake of her head. "Remind me again the next time I try talking to Sean that I should first call and invite Marcy. It's probably for the best if she just pulls up a chair and takes out her notebook. Her imagination is far more exciting than reality."

"So nothing is going on between the two of you?" Molly looked a little disappointed.

Annie gaped at her. "Like I'd have a reason to get back together with the man who broke my heart without any warning!"

Sean had given up everything to please his dad—his mother, this town, her, and all their plans. And Annie—

She stopped herself right there. Because the truth was that Annie had given up everything she loved, too. And in her absence, it had all slipped away.

"Anyway," she said firmly, getting back to the reason for this dinner. "I'm not here to discuss Sean. We need to talk about Dad."

"You spoke with him?" Molly looked nervously at Valerie for a moment. "What did he say?"

"Nothing about Mom, just like you said." Annie shared a collective sigh with her youngest sister.

Valerie, however, just tossed up her hands. "I told you that you wouldn't get anywhere with him. He hasn't opened up about her since the day he moved out. He just spends more time at that office than he already did."

"Well, that might be changing," Annie said. No possibility about it; it was changing. And soon.

"What do you mean?" Molly's face brightened. "Is Dad moving back home?"

Annie's heart sank when she realized she'd have to let her sister down. There was no doubt that Molly wanted their parents to reunite just as much as she did, to go back to big, loud family dinners, and holidays spent decorating a fresh tree and baking in the kitchen for hours, sometimes gathering around the out-of-tune piano so Caroline could put her four years of lessons to use, while they all sang to their favorite carols, often messing up the lyrics.

Would there never be another Christmas like that again? And had Annie missed the last one, being in Seattle?

"We didn't talk about him and Mom," she said carefully, dodging the question, even though she watched Molly's shoulders deflate. "We talked about the paper."

Annie looked around the deck at plenty of familiar faces, people she'd known through passing, old classmates who had stayed put in Harmony Cove rather than moving to Boston or New York like so many had. A few of the shop owners whose businesses she'd frequented since she was a kid.

But no Marcy. When she ever ate out, which wasn't often, she liked to sit in the bar area, where a heavy pour made for more interesting conversation, even if she was just listening rather than engaging in it.

And no Dad. She thought of him back in his office, still working on getting tomorrow's edition to bed, maybe ordering takeout instead of enjoying the perpetually stuffed fridge back at the house, where Annie's mom brought home all the daily leftovers from the café and stored containers of flavorful meals when she was recipe testing.

"Dad told me that he's retiring," Annie said. When silence fell over the table, she looked at each of her sisters' shocked faces and added, "This week."

"What?" Molly gasped.

"This week?" Even Valerie was visibly shocked.

"He thought the timing would work out well, with the paper's centennial celebration." Annie took a long swig of her wine, then motioned to the waiter that they'd need another round. Or, judging from her sisters' expressions, two.

"And he just decided this?" Molly blinked rapidly, looking at Valerie in alarm.

"Who will run the paper?" Valerie asked, getting straight to the point.

"I assume Marcy will," Annie replied, to which an even greater silence ensued. It was a family paper, after all, started by her great-grandfather, and Mitch and Marcy were the last descendants of their generation.

"How will that work?" Molly asked, voicing Annie's unspoken thoughts.

"Did he say what his plans are?" Valerie pressed once the waiter had topped off their glasses and told them that their meals would be out shortly.

"Nope," Annie said.

"You don't think he's planning to move away, do you?" Molly's eyes were wide with alarm. "If he no longer has Mom or the house, and he no longer has the paper, then what will keep him here?"

Annie hadn't considered this possibility, but now she shifted on her chair with unease. She looked at Valerie for guidance, whose furrowed brow indicated that she was worried, too—and that she wasn't pretending otherwise anymore.

"Harmony Cove is Dad's home," Annie said firmly. "He was born here, he raised a family here, and he loves this community."

"But you could say the same things, more or less," Molly pointed out. "And you still left."

It was true, and she had, but at the time she'd needed a change of scenery, to walk into work where she wasn't always looking at a vacant chair that Sean had once occupied. She hadn't intended to make Seattle her forever home, but somewhere along the way, it had become that.

Even if it didn't feel like home at all.

"I left because I had a broken heart," she reminded Molly.

Val's eyebrows shot up. "Exactly my point."

Annie chewed her lower lip, refusing to believe that her father could turn his back on this community. "And I had an opportunity that was too good to pass up," she reminded her sisters. But what they didn't know, because her father could never know, was that the only thing keeping her away was her desire to prove to her father that she was successful—because of him.

And she would be, she reminded herself. Once this article was finished. It was coming along nicely, thanks in part to Sean, who had collected some touching quotes from the locals well in advance of her return. She'd make it shine. She'd get that promotion. And her father could retire feeling fulfilled and happy.

Even if she wasn't so sure that she would ever be.

"We want to throw him a party," Annie said firmly, getting back on track. "Saturday night."

"We?" Val's eyebrows shot up. "Who's *we*?"

"You don't mean Mom, do you?" Molly asked hopefully.

Annie looked at her baby sister for a moment before saying delicately, "No, Mol. I mean..."

Oh, this wasn't going to come out the right way. She tried to think of a way to explain it away, to make it seem less "titillating" as Marcy would say, but it was no use.

"Sean and I," she finished, barely able to look at her sisters, even though she felt their stares as she moved her wineglass around the table.

"You and Sean are planning Dad's retirement party," Val said, struggling to fight off the beginnings of a smile. "My, my. I wonder what Marcy will have to say about this!"

She made a playful show of pulling out her phone and tapping at the screen. Beside her, Molly started to laugh, and despite herself, Annie did, too. She could just picture her aunt perched on her swivel chair, her fingers pounding at the keyboard as her imagination ran wild.

"I suppose there's no use in telling her the only relationship Sean and I have is strictly professional," Annie said with a resigned sigh.

"Is that what you're telling yourself?" Val asked pertly, pushing her phone to the side.

"That's all it is," Annie insisted. And all it ever could be.

But as the conversation stopped when the waiter appeared and they all tucked into their meals, she began to wonder if Val was right—and if Marcy, being the astute observer that she was, might be onto something.

Their cousin Lucy joined them after dinner, and, with the sweet tooth that a baker should have, she insisted on ordering dessert. Over a shared slice of peanut butter chocolate cake, of which Annie admittedly ate most, the sisters filled Lucy in on the plan and tossed around ideas for the party, ranging from a slideshow of their dad's days at the paper to a special edition of the paper for guests only, made up of his best articles over the years.

The photos had already been weeded through and set aside, and off the top of her head, Annie could think of at least a dozen articles that stuck out in her father's tenure, ranging from the profile of the town's retired Santa Claus to the time that the Cape was struck by a particularly bad hurricane, and everyone had pitched in to repair their neighbors' homes. Anything more recent, she might have to ask Marcy for, not revealing her true reason, of course.

"Oh, no," Lucy suddenly said, dropping her fork and hurriedly rubbing any chocolate from her mouth with her napkin. She lowered her chin and pulled half her dark hair down to shield one side of her face. "Don't look now, but Travis Morrison just walked in. He's in the bar area. What if he's coming this way?"

Travis wasn't just Sean's cousin, he was also a notorious flirt, while Lucy had always seemed too sensible to fall for his easy charms.

"Did something happen between the two of you?" Annie asked Lucy, both curious and worried about her cousin.

"No." But Lucy's cheeks had flushed.

"Well, I, for one, hope that he stays away," Val said, looking annoyed.

Annie didn't want to agree, even though she silently did. If Travis was here, there was a real possibility that Sean would soon follow.

"I didn't realize you had a problem with Travis," Lucy said, taking a sip of her wine as she glanced across the deck.

"Oh, you know Travis. He'll just come over and put on the charm, and I don't want to deal with it tonight" was all Val would say with a scoff.

"And I don't want to deal with any Morrison men tonight," Annie said, worried that it might be inevitable.

"Too late," Molly whispered.

Molly looked nearly as anxious as Lucy, and Annie, feeling bold, tossed what she hoped was a discreet glance over her shoulder to see Travis stepping out onto the patio. With Sean.

In jeans and a lightweight sweater that showed off his lean build, he moved with a relaxed gait as if he had been coming to the restaurant every day, not only after disappearing from town for six years.

If Annie didn't know better, she'd say he looked completely at home.

"Hello," she said when he caught her eye and held up his beer.

He grinned until his eyes crinkled and something in her stomach tensed and then rolled over.

"Well, this is a surprise!"

And from the way he had said it, a good one.

Annie, however, wasn't so sure. She'd let her guard down with Sean yesterday, and today she'd hoped to get some space, clear her head, and remind herself that as much as he still looked and acted like the man she'd once intended to spend the rest of her life with, he was also still the man who had an entire career and life waiting for him in DC.

Just like she had in Seattle—sort of.

Travis gave Annie a little smirk and then rested his eyes on Lucy, who squirmed in her chair, unable to stop grinning. "Good evening, ladies. I hope we're not interrupting your dinner."

"Oh, we're finished," Annie said hurriedly, deciding that they would have to forgo the rest of the cake.

"We're just enjoying the ocean breeze and our wine," Val said airily, lifting her glass and sliding Annie a knowing smirk.

"Mind if we pull over some chairs?" Travis asked.

Annie's cheeks burned and she was relieved that it was growing dark. She moved her chair to the right to make room for Sean and Travis—and two of their friends who now approached.

"Mark! Jason!" Annie was happy to see her old classmates—and to know that she wouldn't be forced to spend the evening chatting with Sean while Val flirted with Travis and Molly sat back and observed.

"Annie, it's nice to have you back in town," Mark said, his dimples showing when he bent down to greet her with a hug.

Annie saw Sean's eyes narrow over Mark's shoulder.

When Mark pulled away, she gave him a teasing look. "Not as nice as it is to see you again, Mark. Come and pull up a chair." She motioned to the space between her chair and Valerie's right before Sean could slide in.

She was all too aware of what she was doing, but she also knew that she would rather have Mark sit beside her right now than Sean, who might end up getting the wrong idea. This wasn't a social visit, this was a run-in, and it was supposed to be a girls' night.

Besides, she'd spent enough time with Sean recently.

And she hadn't seen Mark in a while... Not that she'd ever paid much attention to that. Mark Webber was a nice guy, even if he did push her down the slide one too many times on the playground. And steal her swing at recess.

She could overlook childhood mistakes. It was the ones made in adulthood that were more difficult to forgive, she thought, glancing at Sean.

He moved around the table to take a chair opposite hers and next to Molly, who grew quiet in the company of men she wouldn't have remembered from school given the age gap.

Annie asked Mark about his job and his sister, who was a few years ahead of them in school, and who was now married with a baby on the way, and another in preschool. She fawned over the photos of his nephew, admittedly touched Mark's arm a few times when she laughed, and yeah, she might have looked over a few times when she felt the heat of Sean's stare across the table.

He glared at her while he sipped his beer, then eventually turned his attention to Molly, asking her politely about the new seasonal menu items at the café and any of her upcoming summer plans. Eventually, from what Annie could overhear, their conversation settled on an easy topic, which was, of course, Hillary and Tim's engagement.

"I should probably head out," Molly finally said. Now it was Annie's turn to give her sister a suggestive look, but Molly just pulled an apologetic face and explained, "I have to get up at five tomorrow to make muffins for the café."

"They're the best in town," Jason said, making Molly blush.

"It's hard to top the bakery," Travis said, looking Lucy straight in the eye until her cheeks turned a dark shade of pink.

"But the bakery doesn't make muffins," Sean said kindly, giving Molly a wink. "My mother looks forward to your treats every weekend. It's nice to see her smile."

Molly seemed to relax upon hearing those words, and Annie only then remembered how Sean had once been like a big brother to Molly, always a fixture at the dinner table, in the house, or around town. Molly hadn't just been used to him. She'd trusted him. And clearly, she still did.

Molly's grin turned more confident as she gathered her handbag and stood. "It was nice seeing you all."

"I'll drive you back to the house," Annie told her, even if

it was a short walk away and they'd been taking that route on their own since they were kids, running wild all summer with scraped knees and messy ponytails.

"I think I'll head out, too," Sean said suddenly. He pushed his chair back and stood before anyone could respond.

Val gave Annie a funny look, and Mark looked at Annie with mild disappointment when she gathered her handbag and looped it over her shoulder.

"I'll catch a ride with Lucy." Val settled back in her chair with her drink, watching their cousin with protective scrutiny.

"It was nice seeing you guys. We'll have to catch up again next time I'm in town," Annie said, which only reminded her of how far off into the future that would be. With a promotion came more responsibility, meaning more work and more time in the office. In other words, less time here.

The thought of it filled her with dread instead of excitement.

Leaving Valerie and Lucy at the table with the remaining three guys, she started to catch up with Molly, but her sister only turned around once to say, "I'll meet you in the car."

In other words, she was telling Annie that she wasn't going to rescue her from talking to Sean.

Annie would remember this come Christmastime. A lump of coal might be in order.

She watched as Molly quickened her pace across the gravel parking lot, knowing that she couldn't catch up without all but jogging.

"Thanks for that," she said in a low voice that only Sean

would hear. "For sort of saving Molly back there. She can get shy sometimes."

He brushed away the gratitude. "She's always been the kid sister I never had. You know how much I care about her. About all of you."

Annie swallowed hard. She did know it. She just didn't know how to feel about it. Or how it changed anything.

"I hope that my cousin doesn't fall for Travis." She glanced up at Sean and added, "No offense."

"None taken." Sean stuffed his hands into his pockets. "What can I say? *My* cousin has a way with the ladies. From the looks of it, he's not the only one..."

Annie had to bite her lip to hide her smile.

"What's that supposed to mean?" She tipped her head.

"I mean, I didn't realize that you were ever interested in Mark Webber," Sean said, his jaw twitching.

Annie laughed. "Mark? We're just two old friends catching up, Sean. Besides, you and I aren't dating anymore, so why should you care who I talk to...or date, for that matter?"

"I don't, I mean, I do, I do care...about you." Sean huffed out a breath. "I don't even know who you're friends with, who you date, or what you've been up to."

"Well, you sort of lost that right when you walked out of this town and my life six years ago and never looked back," Annie pointed out, an edge creeping into her tone.

Sean pressed his lips together. "Fair enough. Let me take you to dinner, then, so we can properly catch up."

Alarm bells went off in Annie's head, and she knew that the pounding of her heart should be panic, not...excitement.

"Dinner?" As in...a date?

"Lunch, then. Nothing formal," Sean clarified. "Casual. Just...two old friends getting reacquainted." His mouth quirked into a smile, and damn him if her heart didn't then start to flutter a little.

Two old friends. Catching up.

She should say no, but her heart said yes, because as much as she wanted to stay angry at Sean, he kept making that impossible.

"I can do that," she said.

Only as she turned and hurried to catch up with her sister, she wasn't sure that she could do that, any more than she was sure that she and Sean could ever only be two old friends.

Eight

A lunch date. With Sean. Annie was happy that Valerie was booked with dog walks and Molly was busy at the café as she rode her bike through town, past the shops and the people out enjoying the warm spring day. Tulips were popping up, the sun was warm on her face, and by all other accounts, it had the promise of a beautiful day—but she was careful not to get too carried away.

Sean had a way of disappointing her when she least expected it. She couldn't let herself get swept up in the moment.

Especially when a moment was all they had.

The ride to the beach wasn't short, but she enjoyed the salty breeze on her face as she took the path out of town and toward the Atlantic, remembering all the days that she and her sisters—and later she and Sean—would take this same route on lazy summer days, eager to settle in for an afternoon on the sand, or to splash around in the surf and later dry off on towels, side by side, hand in hand.

He was already waiting for her at the seaside snack shop that was a local favorite, wearing a grin that always won her over and she knew why—he'd secured the best table, the one with the unobstructed view of the water. Their table, was how she'd come to think of it.

How they both had.

It both pained her and touched her to realize that he remembered that, too. That they shared a past. Memories. An entire chapter of their lives that would forever be intertwined and could never be undone.

And maybe might best be not forgotten, after all.

Lowering her guard, but not too much, she scooted onto the bench. This place was as casual as it got in Harmony Cove, with its weather-worn picnic tables that sat on a stretch of sand open to the elements with a vast view of the Atlantic. The wind was low today, and the beachfront was mostly empty aside from a few surfers who never took a day off. Gulls circled above, squawking and calling, hoping to catch a table scrap or that a child would ignore the signs advising against feeding the birds.

"I took the liberty of ordering for us in case they ran out," Sean told her.

"Good," Annie said, relieved. It was known to happen; it made for some mighty disappointed customers who flocked for the overstuffed lobster rolls, but it also drew them in all the more. She wasn't sure if it was a marketing ploy or a supply issue. Either way, her stomach turned over with anticipation—or nerves.

In a casual T-shirt, Sean certainly hadn't made much of an effort for this date, but he looked just as good—or better

—than if he'd been sporting a tux. Her gaze trailed from his chiseled jaw to his well-defined biceps, to the hands that used to touch her skin, tracing patterns, making her writhe with pleasure.

Feeling Sean's eyes on hers, she cleared her throat and said, "I told my sisters about the party. And...about the retirement twist."

"How'd that go?" he asked.

Annie thought about it for a minute and then said, "Once the shock wore off, they seemed supportive. They had some great ideas." She told him about their suggestion to create a special edition of their father's best articles before getting to the burning question. "You don't think...I mean, my father hasn't mentioned... Do you think he plans to leave Harmony Cove?"

Sean frowned deeply. "I haven't gotten that impression, why?"

Annie was only partially comforted by his response. "Molly made a good point that without my mom and the paper, there might not be any reason to stay. Maybe he's retiring because of the separation. Maybe this is his way to kickstart the next chapter of his life."

Sean's brows knitted together as the waitress approached and set two iced teas on the tables. He sipped his drink thoughtfully, but he shook his head firmly when he set the plastic cup back on the table.

"No. I don't think your father has plans to move. And wouldn't he have told you if he did?"

Once, Annie might have thought so, but now, she didn't know what to think.

"He didn't tell me about my mother kicking him out of the house," she pointed out. "And he hasn't told anyone else about his retirement yet, at least not that I'm aware of."

"Maybe he's having second thoughts," Sean said.

They sat in hopeful silence until Annie shook her head. They both knew that Mitch Baker was not just a man of his word but a man who used his words carefully. He never would have told Annie he was retiring unless he intended to do just that.

"Without the house and the paper and his marriage, I'm not sure he has much reason to stay," Annie sighed.

"But this town means everything to him," Sean pointed out.

"Just because something means everything to you doesn't mean you can't let it go," she said, feeling her heart pull tight as their eyes met.

He was the first to look away. "This town means something to you."

"Everything," she said, thinking of her empty apartment back in Seattle. Sure, she had some friends who she'd met through work, but they only knew the woman who had shown up in a strange city and was determined to bury herself in the job—first to escape the pain of missing Sean, and later to convince herself that she had made the right decision.

She cleared her throat, her father's words coming back to her in a rush, the gleam of pride in his eyes making her stomach roll over.

"But life can pull us away and keep us away. Look at Caroline," she said. Then, realizing that Sean might not be privy to that gossip unless he'd read about it in the Harmony Happenings column, she said, "You heard that my sister's ex-fiancé is now engaged to our cousin Hillary?"

His mouth twitched. "You do remember that I work with Marcy, right?"

Annie sputtered on a sip of her drink. Point made.

"I still can't believe that Tim would do that to Caroline," Sean said with narrowed eyes and a shake of the head.

"Well, believe it," Annie said, even though she'd struggled to do just that when she'd been there the day that Tim's brother walked into the church and told them all that Tim wasn't coming.

"But they were together for years," Sean insisted.

Annie stared at him. Hard. "Sometimes a shared past isn't enough to create a future."

He lowered his eyes. Point taken.

"I guess I missed a lot," Sean finally said after a beat of silence. "My mom isn't one to gossip, and the only other person I ever really kept in touch with was my cousin. And Travis has more important matters to discuss than other people's love lives."

He gave her a little smile, one that she knew was meant to ease the tension between them that still came up every time she thought of their history.

"Well, the gist of it is that Tim didn't even have the decency to call off the wedding, he had Lucas do it for him while he slid off to Boston, where he remained until recently, it would seem. He never even explained to Caroline why he couldn't go through with it. A few days later, Caroline packed up and left town. She hasn't been back since." Annie knew that her heartache was no match for Caroline's, but sitting here across from Sean, talking to him so easily, made her long for those days when he was hers and she was his and they were always together.

And, she thought, always would be.

Oh, sure, there hadn't been a proposal. They were twenty-four, he'd just finished grad school at his father's insistence, and she assumed the next step was coming. Knew it was coming, really. They'd been together for seven years. They had a plan to make a name for themselves right here in the place they loved most, with the person they loved most, and up until that point, they'd followed it, both getting into the same program at the same college, working at the paper on summer breaks. They loved Harmony Cove, and they loved each other.

She'd thought it would be enough.

But as her mother had said, sometimes love just wasn't enough.

"He didn't say why he changed his mind?" Sean asked.

Annie gave him a hard stare, one that she hoped conveyed to him that they weren't talking about her sister and Tim anymore.

"Does the reason even matter?" she finally said wearily. In her case, it didn't. Sean had explained himself, her older self understood, but that didn't take the hurt away. And it didn't change the circumstances.

"Anyway." Annie squeezed a wedge of lemon into her iced tea. "Caroline moved to get a fresh start. I guess that Molly is worried our dad will do the same."

"Talk to him, then," Sean suggested. "He's always been honest with you."

Always expected the most from her, too, she wanted to say, but she knew that wouldn't be fair. Her father just wanted the best for her, worked hard to give her every opportunity, and then he shone with pride when she succeeded, feeling like he had accomplished something, too. But Sean's father just wanted his sons to follow in his footsteps, to love what he loved, even if they loved something else.

Or maybe someone else.

Annie's eyes met Sean's across the table, and she felt the pull of their shared past, a connection, and an emotion that they'd once had for each other—and maybe hadn't forgotten.

The waitress reappeared again, this time with two baskets of lobster rolls and fries. Annie couldn't help but lick her lips.

"I should have probably ordered two." Sean laughed as he dug into his food. "Or maybe we'll just have to do this again sometime."

Sometime. Annie felt her smile fade, her good spirits replaced by cold reality. When would that time be? The next time she returned to Harmony Cove? And would Sean still be here then? To ask would bring up the sensitive topic of his mother, and she didn't want to do that, so instead she took a small and slow bite of the roll, savoring the sweet and creamy taste.

"This beats the one at the ferry stop," she said.

"They must have good seafood in Seattle," Sean commented, popping a fry into his mouth.

"Oh, sure, but it's not the same. Nothing's the same," she said, hearing the sadness in her tone.

Sean must have picked up on it because he stopped eating to glance at her. "Tell me about Seattle. What's your apartment like? Your coworkers? Friends?"

Boyfriends? She could practically hear the unspoken word.

"Oh, work keeps me busy…" If working on a joyless column and occasionally having drinks across the street from the office counted as busy. "My apartment is walking distance from the paper, so I don't need a car. It's as rainy as you'd expect."

He nodded along politely while she tried to think of a way to describe how she'd spent the last four years of her life.

"My coworkers are friendly." And they were. But they were also all married now. She'd gone to most of their weddings. Several of them were starting families. The only reason she was even up for a promotion was because Trina Daniels had decided to stay home full-time with her newborn son. What would her father have to say about that—or if she didn't get the better job at all?

Annie had dared to hope that this promotion might be the opening she was waiting for—the chance to feel inspired again, to be excited about the place she'd traded for the Cape.

But being back in Harmony Cove after a year and a half away only reminded her that this was where she felt most alive. And most like herself.

"So you like your job?" Sean's head was tipped, and he was staring at her thoughtfully, giving her his full attention. A reporter's face, she thought.

She couldn't help but smile, because it was almost funny. "I do," she said, even though she really, really didn't. "And your job must be exciting."

His eyes went flat as he nodded. "Busy, and exciting for some. But it's tiring to travel as much as I do, and there isn't a lot of time for anything outside of work."

They both went back to their food for a while, commenting on how good it was and how much they had missed it.

But it wasn't just the lobster she missed, and from the downcast look in Sean's eyes, she wondered if it was more than that for him, too.

She'd missed this. The two of them, the salty air, and the sun on her face. The knowledge that the people she loved most were just down the road and that she didn't have to pack a bag or book a flight to give them a hug. She missed waking up to the smell of the coffee percolating in the kitchen and seeing her father on the back porch when she came downstairs, the morning paper in his hand even though he knew every article.

She missed the life she used to have.

"Remind me never to stay away this long again," Annie said.

"Easy," Sean said through a mouthful of lobster. "Don't ever stay away this long again."

Their eyes met across the table, and Annie felt her breath catch as her heart tugged in her chest. She blinked quickly and looked away, forcing herself to continue chewing, this time not tasting a thing.

"So...you leave for Seattle on Sunday, then?" Sean asked when their food was finished.

Annie nodded. "Yep."

Her time here was now halfway over. It seemed almost impossible to believe how much had occurred since she'd stepped off that ferry. How laughable it was that she was sitting here, on a warm spring day, across from Sean of all people right now.

But she was. And it felt comfortable. And nice. And sort of bittersweet.

They weren't the same people they'd been the last time they'd sat at this table.

They'd gone their separate ways, life had happened, changed them, thrown them a few curve balls, especially recently, and now here they were. Two people with a shared past and some real challenges. They understood each other in ways no one else could.

And that was what made it so hard to think about saying goodbye for a second time.

"I'm sure everyone will be happy to have you back," Sean said.

Annie couldn't imagine who, but she nodded.

Sean took a sip of his drink and leaned into the table on his elbows as he watched the waves crash against the shore for a moment. "Anyone, um, in particular?"

Annie fought off a grin. So he *was* wondering if she was seeing anyone. She knew she shouldn't be flattered by this but she couldn't help it. He had broken her heart, after all. Let him miss her a bit. Served him right.

"Not at the moment," she said vaguely.

He looked at her with noticeable relief, and this time, they did share a grin.

Annie knew that she shouldn't care, but she saw an opportunity to ask a question and the journalist in her knew that it might not present itself again. "And you? Anyone special in your life?"

"Me?" Sean seemed taken aback by the question. "It's all work and no play for me. Besides, I'm never in one place long enough to get to know someone."

Including here, she thought.

It was a firm reminder that she couldn't let her heart soften to him, not when nothing had changed between them. He was still the guy who could pick up and leave at any moment, and chances were that he would, whenever his mother recovered, or worse.

That these past few days when she'd let him back into her life, however professionally, meant nothing, and certainly changed even less.

That she'd be wise to keep her distance.

"Well," she said, pushing back from the picnic table. "This was a nice lunch, but I should probably head out if I'm going to get to my interview with Wally Thompson. He's promised me some juicy stories about his morning fishing trips with my dad."

"Sounds riveting." Sean grinned as he tossed a few bills on the table and stood up. "I have some notes to share with you, too. I talked with Marcy this morning. She told me some great stories about coming into the office with their father."

Annie's grandfather. She smiled at the memory of the

man she hadn't known for long before a heart attack cut his life short. "Dad probably told me these stories once, but it will be good to get another perspective."

She and Sean exchanged a glance and laughed. Marcy certainly knew how to spin a story.

Annie walked over to the bike rack and balanced her cruiser. "Did you ride over?"

Sean looked disappointed. "I drove."

Once again, they were at a crossroads, and it was time to go their separate ways.

"I'll probably see you at the office tomorrow. I want to go through some of my dad's old articles."

He nodded but didn't move.

The street was quiet, and they were the only ones on the sidewalk. In another lifetime, they would have reached out, held hands, and walked home to a little shingled cottage together.

Maybe they would have had a kid by now, or maybe they'd just be dreaming of the ones that they would.

But instead, Sean gave her a sad sort of smile and said, "I'll see you later, Annie."

And with a resigned nod, she climbed onto her bike and pedaled away, just like she wanted to do. Only not like she'd wanted at all.

The light was on in the kitchen when Sean arrived home late that night, after putting in extra time on his article after his coworkers had left for the day and the office was quiet.

Conflicting emotions from his lunch with Annie still lingered in his chest, making each step heavier than the next.

Once, he would have expected to see his mother sitting at the kitchen table with a cup of tea and a book—she'd always loved a good mystery novel, even though she complained that they kept her up far too long into the night—but now he knew better. His mother was rarely awake past six most days, and that was on a good day, and those were fewer and farther in between.

He started to head for the stairs, but the creaking floors drew his father's attention from the back of the house.

"Sean?" the deep voice called out. "That you?"

Who else would it be? Drew couldn't even be bothered to come back for a weekend visit.

With a heavy sigh, Sean closed his eyes and then forced his way down the hallway.

"Hey, Dad." He saw his father sitting on the back patio, a glass of scotch in his hand. No books or newspaper in front of him.

Alone with his thoughts, it would seem.

Or maybe his conscience.

"Care for one?" Sean's father motioned to the decanter on the bar cart.

Sean nodded begrudgingly. One wouldn't hurt, though he'd rather go upstairs and shut the door.

He poured a small amount into a tumbler and pulled out a chair.

"Nice night," he said, trying to keep the tone light. Small talk with his father was best, he'd learned. Other than that, they didn't have much in common. His dad had Drew for that. His dad had Drew for everything.

"Busy day?" his father asked.

Sean nodded but kept the details to himself. He knew his father wouldn't approve of him spending time with Annie any more than the piece he was writing on Mitch's legacy. The way Bill Morrison saw it, the Bakers would only hold Sean back.

"When you get back to DC—" his father began.

"Who said I'm going back to DC?" Sean asked.

His father gave him a long, cold stare. It was a warning look. It was a look that Sean knew far too well.

Normally, Sean's mother would try to break them apart at this point, before things got worse, but Sean's mother was upstairs resting right now. She wasn't here to intervene.

Soon, she wouldn't be here at all.

Sean took a longer sip of the drink. It burned its way down his throat.

"They're holding your position. And you have no reason to stay here," his father said firmly.

"Maybe I have no reason to leave," Sean replied evenly. "You ever think about it like that?"

"What do you mean, you have no reason to leave?" Bill's voice rose with emotion.

"I mean, that I have a perfectly good job right here in Harmony Cove," Sean said, bracing himself.

He watched his father's eyes grow with anger. "That's a temporary job, Sean, so you don't look like you're out of work."

Yes, because heaven forbid Sean was ever out of work, no

matter how extenuating the circumstances. His father still clocked a full ten hours a day at the office, after all.

"You work on the Cape," Sean pointed out, knowing that he was asking for a fight now, and not caring.

"I run a law firm," his father all but spat. "One that can afford this house." He spread his arms wide, showing off the large backyard with the custom-built pool, turning to reveal the back of the cedar-shingled five-bedroom house.

"It's all about money to you, isn't it?" Sean said, taking a slower sip of his drink.

"And what is it to you, Sean? What is work if not for money? For what money can buy? Fun? Mental stimulation? That's called a hobby. Or charity. Either of which you can do in your spare time."

"How about making a difference? Or fulfillment?" Sean countered. He slanted a glance at his father and held it there. "Life is short, Dad. You of all people should know that."

"So you're saying what?" Bill ground out. "That you're considering staying on here, in this town, at that paper?" The way he nearly spat the words said everything about what he thought about the *Herald*.

"Why not?" Sean asked now, just as he had then. Everything about this conversation was nearly identical to the one he'd had six years ago, only then Annie had been a factor, and another one for his father to dismiss.

"After all we've done for you!" his father shouted, his face turning red. "We gave you everything! A college education! Graduate school! Opportunities that not everyone has! I had to pay my way through college, working night shifts during law school! And this is how you repay your mother and me? By throwing it all in our faces?"

"I don't think working hard at a job I love is throwing it all in your face. And I would think that as my parents, you'd want to see me happy," Sean replied, knowing that he was fighting a losing battle.

"Happy!" Bill tossed his hands in the air. "Do you hear how selfish you sound? Now Drew! There's a son who appreciates all that we've done for him. There's a boy who made the most of the opportunities he was given."

Who made him proud.

Sean knew. He knew all too well.

"You always preferred Drew, even when we were kids," Sean said, managing to keep the emotion from rising in his voice. Or maybe there just wasn't any left.

"You would say that," his father grumbled, taking another swig of his drink.

"What's that supposed to mean?" Sean asked.

"It means that you're looking for excuses to avoid taking responsibility," his father said, glaring at him. "For why you fell short."

Fell short. So he was admitting it. Loud and clear.

"What was it about Drew, Dad? Was it that he was captain of the football team, while I was on the bench half the season? Or was it that he followed in your profession, while I had other interests?"

"Drew is driven." Bill stared out at the pool. "He always was, even as a boy. Whatever he wanted, he committed himself and he succeeded."

"And I didn't?" Sean asked. "I committed myself to the paper. To Annie."

"Did you?" His father raised an eyebrow.

"Oh, now that's not fair." Sean set down his glass before he did something stupid. He felt his temper rise like never before.

"Drew reached high."

"I don't call what I wanted reaching low," Sean said icily. "But I always fell short with you."

"That's because Drew has his priorities in order!" Bill made a fist and pounded the side of his deck chair, causing it to shake.

"His priorities?" Sean shot back. He stared at his father in disbelief. "Drew hasn't been back for more than a weekend in two months, Dad. Our mother is dying, and he can't take time off work to visit her."

"He's holding down the Boston office so I can be here with your mother. She understands how important the firm is and how hard he's worked to be the success that he is. She wouldn't want him to give up on his dreams and his opportunities."

No, only Sean was expected to do that.

"People take time off from work all the time, Dad. I did," Sean pointed out.

"He has a big trial to prepare for—"

Sean gave a bitter laugh and stood to go back into the house. He didn't even know why he was having this conversation. He and his father would never see eye to eye.

And he was done trying to make that happen.

Nine

Annie woke to the smell of coffee and the sound of laughter. For a moment, she lay completely still under the blankets, wondering if the past week had all just been a bad dream. She strained for the sounds of her father's voice coming from the rooms below, but all she heard were the voices of Valerie and Molly, pots clambering against the stovetop, and cabinet doors opening and closing.

It wasn't the same. But maybe, she thought with newfound hope, it was close enough.

Pushing herself out of bed, she tossed a sweatshirt over her T-shirt and went down the creaking stairs, rounding the hallway into the kitchen where the Baker women were moving about the large room like a well-choreographed dance.

Annie held back, leaning against the doorframe, letting herself be taken back to all those mornings she'd both cherished and taken for granted, the ones that were so ingrained in their family that there was never a thought that they might suddenly end.

"Oh, Annie, you're up!" Her mother turned from the oven, where she was retrieving a tray of her famous French toast casserole, which was a glorified bread pudding, oozing with brown sugar and cinnamon.

"I didn't know we were having a family breakfast." Annie moved into the kitchen to take a mug of coffee from Molly.

"I already prepped at the café and my team can handle things for a few hours on their own," Sharon replied as she dusted the casserole with powdered sugar. "I wasn't going to let you leave town without taking some time off to spend with you."

"Mom, I could have made breakfast for you," Annie insisted, even as her stomach grumbled.

"What can I say?" Sharon began spooning the decadent breakfast onto plates. "I love what I do. When you follow your passion, it's not work. It's love."

Annie wanted to point out that the same could be said for her father, who used to say that he had never worked a day in his life, but she knew now that her mother had some complicated feelings about the hours that Mitch put in at the paper, so she kept her mouth closed—or at least, full of warm and sweet French toast.

"See, this is why I can't come back to town more often," Annie said. "I'd gain twenty pounds!"

"And that is why you aren't allowed to come back more often," Valerie said, taking a large bite. "Mom only makes this for special occasions."

"And today is one of them," Sharon sighed with contentment as she scooted her chair into the table.

"You must walk at least ten miles a day," Molly said to Val. "And if you call this temptation, imagine working at the café. I don't know if it's such a bad thing that I rarely have time to sit down and eat most days."

"The café is still going strong, then." Annie had no reason to think otherwise, but given the changes at the newspaper, she couldn't help but be worried about their family's other cherished business.

"As busy as ever," Sharon said proudly. Without the makeup or wardrobe from Sandra's boutique, for a moment, she looked like her old self again. "Not that I would use it as an excuse to skip a family gathering. Only one person is missing," she added with a sigh.

"Dad?" Annie blurted before she caught the alarm in Val's face across the table, and she immediately realized she had misspoken.

Molly tittered nervously behind her oversized mug, and their mother took a moment to recover before giving Annie a look of surprise. "Caroline."

Of course. The leader of the pack. Caroline's absence was noticeable, and not just because of her empty chair. With their cousins' engagement party tomorrow, Annie knew that she was on everyone's mind.

She just hoped that Marcy knew better than to post anything about it in the next article. It was entirely likely that Caroline was reading a digital copy of the *Herald* from afar; it was their father's paper, after all.

For now.

"Caroline will come home when she's ready," Val said with more confidence than Annie felt. She took the last bite of her food and stood. "I'd better hurry over to the Levinsons' before Peanut chews up the throw pillows again. When he's left on his own for too long, he gets spiteful."

"Isn't Peanut a dog?" Annie said, remembering the Lab owned by the husband and wife real estate agents, who worked mostly evenings and weekends.

Val just raised an eyebrow. "Dogs can be as vengeful as cats, Annie. I have one little guy who lifts his leg to the vacuum if it's not put in the closet because he hates the sound of it."

Everyone laughed, and Annie watched her mother's eyes crinkle with amusement. Had she shown that same genuine reaction the other night when they were all out at the bistro? Annie didn't think so. It had been a different kind of energy then, as if her mother was searching for something rather than just enjoying the moment.

"What do you all have going on today?" Val carried her plate to the sink and rinsed it.

"I was thinking of going to the garden center if I can steal some time from the café," Molly said. "I thought I'd get some more tomato plants for the garden. I have a feeling we'll be making a lot of gazpacho this summer."

"Excellent idea," Sharon said with a nod. "I'll join you if you're willing to wait until closing time."

"Actually," Annie cut in. "I was thinking that we could spend a little time together, Mom. Maybe go shopping when you're done with work? I didn't bring anything to wear to the party."

Or parties, now that there was the engagement party for Hillary and the retirement party for her father. She'd need two dresses, unless she wanted to wiggle into something belonging to one of her sisters, who were both a full dress size smaller than her, though she didn't know how, given their mother's cooking.

Although, maybe these types of family meals had ended along with her parents' relationship.

"Oh, that does sound fun," Sharon agreed, the idea seeming to grow on her. "And I have been wanting to get some new clothes for the warmer weather."

Nothing too pink, Annie could only hope.

"You're welcome to join us," Annie said to Molly, who quickly shook her head.

"Oh, no, you two go and have fun. I'm with Mom every day. It's your turn now." Molly smiled sweetly but there was a gleam in her eyes.

From across the room, Annie thought she heard Val snort before the screen door banged shut behind her. She supposed that Molly did bear the brunt of their parents' fallout, and it couldn't be easy on her working with their mother at the café all day and knowing that there was nothing she could say to make things better.

"In fact, why don't I cover the café for the day," Molly went on. "You'll just be down the street if anything comes up, and that way the two of you could spend some quality time together."

"Some quality time is just what we need," Annie said to her mother, feeling certain that by the time the afternoon was through, her mother would have come to her senses.

Or at least agree to attend their father's party.

Two hours later, Annie stood outside the dressing room door of her aunt Sandra's boutique, her arms full of skirts, shorts, blouses, and dresses in every shade of pink. From behind the velvet curtain, there was a rustle, and a moment later, her mother whisked out into the storefront in yet another magenta dress.

"Lovely!" Sandra cried, clasping her hands together. "I think this is the one, Shar."

Shar? Was this a new nickname to go with the new look?

Annie's mother studied herself in a full-length mirror as she smoothed the fabric at her hips. She did a little turn, looking coquettishly over her shoulder, before, to Annie's horror, pursing her lips.

"I swear, it takes ten years off you," Sandra said as she came to stand beside Annie, who had been hanging back near a table of lightweight sweaters, waiting for the right moment to suggest one. "Doesn't your mother look great, Annie? The best you've looked in years, Shar."

Annie gritted her teeth. Sandra, in her form-revealing clothes that she forever hoped would help her gain the attention of middle-aged bachelors and summer tourists, though never, to her disappointment, permanently, seemed thrilled that her older sister had finally shed her practical jeans and sensible pullovers for a flashier look.

Annie, however, didn't share her aunt's enthusiasm. Or her style. What could she say? She liked the way her mother's hair had always been, blond, and in recent years with streaks of gray. She preferred the faded jeans and soft sweaters, and the simple jewelry, if any at all. Her mother didn't need all that makeup; it only covered up her natural good features.

But Sandra was practically levitating and *Shar* was giddy as she turned this way and that in the three-way mirror.

The dress *was* a flattering cut, and the shade of pink was not entirely terrible, but Annie would not go so far as to say that her mother looked the best she had in years. Far from it.

"Ravishing, simply ravishing," Sandra gushed, and this time Annie tossed her aunt a glare. If Sandra caught it, she pretended not to notice, instead turning to riffle through the costume jewelry display case near the front counter of the small shop that she'd run since her divorce. "I have the perfect necklace to draw attention to your face."

Out came a thick rhinestone necklace. Sandra wrapped it around her sister's neck like a snake.

"You don't think it's too much?" Sharon touched her collarbone uncertainly.

"Nonsense!" Sandra clucked, making Sharon almost wilt and Annie roll her eyes to the ceiling. "You're done with all that boring beige and understated gold jewelry. If you want people to notice you, you have to give them a reason to look."

Annie sputtered on a cough. "And who are you hoping will notice you, Mom?"

Her mother stared blankly at her as the room fell silent. Finally, Sandra said, "Men, darling. Your mother is in her prime! This is her time and she needs to seize it!"

Oh, how Annie wished her aunt Kathy was here, but of

course her other, more sensible aunt was busy at the inn tending to guests or tucked away in the adjacent bakery, mixing cookie dough or frosting a cake, not playing dress-up with her middle-aged sisters.

"Why don't we get a coffee, Mom?" Annie suggested, eager to get out of this store, which seemed to be stocking more pink than she remembered in the past. "I could use some caffeine."

Or a drink, but seeing as it wasn't even noon yet, she'd pass on that.

"Shall I ring this up?" Sandra asked when Annie's mother slipped back into the dressing room.

From behind the curtain, Sharon called, "Yes, and I think I'll take that sweater you're holding, Annie. The one with the low neckline?"

Of course. How could Annie forget?

"Are you sure, Mom?" she asked warily as Sandra scooped the clothes from her arms and gathered the remaining few that were flung over the curtain rod.

"Of course I'm sure! You heard Sandra! That sweater makes me look ten years younger!"

And so did the dress, apparently. And everything else that Sandra was happily scanning into her computer system. That sales tactic might work for Sandra with some of her other customers, but Annie could see right through it.

"I think I'll wear that sweater today, Sandy," her mother said, falling back on childhood pet names. "As you keep telling me, there's no time like the present!"

"And no sense living in the past!" Sandra said firmly, giving Annie a wink.

Annie gave a nervous smile. Was her aunt referring to her relationship with Sean or her mother's marriage to her father?

Giggling like a girl far below her age, Sandra grabbed the sweater from the top of the pile, slid it through the crack in the curtain, and then handed over a package of something she promised would enhance the look.

Annie didn't even want to know what it could be.

"What about your nice blue dress?" Annie said through the curtain, remembering the elegant outfit that her mother had worn for Caroline's rehearsal dinner. "That would be perfect for Hillary's party."

"That old thing?" her mother tutted.

"And wouldn't that be bad luck, dear?" Sandra eyed Annie. "We don't want anything to jeopardize Hillary's big day."

"You must be excited to see one of your daughters get married," she told her aunt diplomatically. It was a messy situation, but Sandra didn't seem to notice when she beamed broadly.

"If I have any say in it, it's going to be the wedding of Hillary's dreams. And mine," she added with a laugh.

Annie wondered if Tim Reynolds was capable of going through with this marriage when he couldn't commit to her sister, but she saw the worry in her aunt's eyes behind the big smile and said nothing.

Besides, how could she speak when her mother had just yanked back the curtain to show off her new sweater? Annie tried not to gape—or stare—but it was impossible when she realized that her mother must have put on more than the sweater in there because her bust was at least twice the usual size.

"Magic every time," Sandra said with a smile in her voice from the counter. "Makes a *huge* difference."

Huge was the correct word, all right.

"Now, let me total this up for you," Sandra said gaily. "Family discount, of course."

Of course. Sharon was probably Sandra's best customer these days, or at least her most gullible. Annie waited until they were back on the sidewalk to grab her mother's elbow and say, "I don't know who's enjoying your new marital status more. You or Sandra."

"Annie!" For a moment, Sharon looked so horrified that Annie felt momentarily shamed. "Sandra knows what it's like to be single. She's been a huge help to me these past few months."

Annie knew that this was probably true. Sandra had been on her own since before Hillary started school and none of the relationships she'd had since then had turned into something more.

"We're just having a little fun," Sharon assured her.

There was that word again. And Annie could think of at least one person who was not having any fun, and that was her dad.

"I'm just worried about you, Mom," Annie said gently. She knew more than anyone how easy it was to say that you were fine when you weren't.

"That's a mother's job," Sharon said, linking her arm and giving her a little pat. "Tell me, what are you eating in Seattle? Are you getting enough vitamin D?"

Annie laughed and let the conversation shift to more neutral territory as they went in search of coffee and someplace to sit. The town's only designated coffee shop was just ahead, and while she normally preferred to get her drinks at the café, she was more than happy to support other local businesses.

Becky Perkins, her friend who had taken over the business from her grandparents when they graduated from high school, greeted Annie with a big hug when they approached the counter.

"Back at last!" she exclaimed. "How long has it been this time?"

"Too long." For more reasons than usual, Annie wished that she kept in better touch with Becky. Not only was she warm and funny, but she certainly would have filled Annie in about some of the relevant news in town.

"I'll say," Becky said, giving a little waggle of her eyebrows as she stepped back around the counter. "I know Marcy's been counting the days for your return ever since Sean moved back to town."

Annie found little amusement in this, but it at least brought a smile to her mother's heavily painted lips.

"Sean and Annie. Now there's a couple I thought would last," she said with a wistful sigh.

"I can think of another," Annie said, giving her mother a hard stare.

Becky, meanwhile, was busy chatting about the weather, the seasonal changes to her menu, and, of course, who could forget Sharon's sweater?

"That is a beautiful sweater," she remarked as she

prepared their orders: two vanilla lattes, extra sweet for Annie's, and an extra shot, too. "I tried it on last week, but I didn't think I could pull it off."

Few could, Annie thought.

Sure enough, Sharon's cheeks flushed and her eyes filled with joy so obvious that Annie was again ashamed for not finding their little romp in the boutique more fulfilling.

"Thank you!" she exclaimed, setting a hand to her obvious decolletage.

Even Becky's gaze rested there for a moment before she recovered and began preparing their orders.

Just then Justine Winters pushed through the door; she must have been opening her summer home early this year. She walked right past them to the counter and then stopped to do a double take. "Sharon? Sharon Baker? Why, I barely recognized you!"

They quickly hugged and Justine stood back, holding Annie's mother at arm's length with her tanned arms from her winter home in Palm Beach. "You look *fabulous*! What brought on this transformation?"

Did Justine really want to know? Annie stared at her mother with bated breath, but much to her relief, Sharon just grinned and said, "I thought it was time for a new look."

Annie exchanged a sympathetic glance with Becky, who quickly went back to foaming milk for their drinks.

"You'll have to take me shopping with you one of these days," Justine gushed, which was a little less sincere, considering her designer wardrobe. "I could use a makeover, too. Though, I swear, most days, I feel like I could come down the stairs wearing nothing but an apron and I don't think Hank would look up from his paper."

Sharon snorted. "If it's the *Harmony Herald*, then I feel your pain. I lost my husband to that rag years ago."

At this, Annie saw Becky's eyes widen over the espresso machine.

Was this true? Annie sidestepped, not wanting to bear witness to the harsh realities of what she now deemed to be her parents' less-than-perfect marriage, and nearly fell backward when her heel hit something.

"Whoa," Sean said, steadying her by the elbows. "Careful there or you'll spill your coffee."

"Good thing I don't have any yet," Annie said, brushing a strand of hair from her forehead.

Her cheeks flamed when she realized she had tripped over his shoe, and worse, that her mother, Justine, and even Becky were watching the entire exchange with unabashed interest.

"Sean! We were just talking about you!" Annie's mother blurted.

"Will it be your usual today, Sean?" Becky quickly cut in. Bless her.

"The usual would be great, thanks." Sean nodded at Becky behind the counter and then slanted a glance at Sharon.

Annie watched Sean carefully, with keen interest, wondering if he'd be able to keep his gaze from dropping, and she struggled not to laugh as his eyes widened but never left her mother's face. If she didn't know better, she'd say that he didn't even dare to blink.

"It's so nice to see you, Sharon," Sean said, then cleared his throat. "It's...uh...been a while."

Becky could barely suppress her giggles as she slid the paper cups across the counter to Annie, who hid her smile behind her to-go cup.

"Next time you come into Sweet Harmony, stop by the kitchen and say hello," Sharon told him, sliding Annie a glance. "No need to be shy around me."

"Thanks, I, uh..." To Annie's delight, Sean gulped.

Wait. Was that sweat beading on his forehead? It was, it definitely was, and considering the front door was open, and it was a cool spring day, it had absolutely nothing to do with the temperature.

Annie watched him squirm a little more. Her mother kept her head tilted, waiting patiently for his excuse.

"I didn't want to make things awkward," he finally said.

As if anything could be more awkward than this.

Annie couldn't even look at Becky or she'd completely lose it. She could see that her friend was relieved when Justine stepped forward to place her order and she had something else to focus on for a bit.

"Nonsense!" Sharon was saying as she brushed a hand through the air. "You're always welcome in the café. And you and Annie seem to be getting along."

She tossed a suggestive glance at Annie, who stifled a sigh.

"I'm sure you've heard about the article we're working on," he said, nodding along, still fighting to keep his eyes level with hers, not half an inch lower.

"Ah, yes, the article." Sharon's lips thinned.

It wasn't until now that Annie realized how her mother might feel about the article, but surely she couldn't argue that a family paper lasting one hundred years in this new digital era was not only newsworthy but inspirational?

"It's a nod to yesteryear," Annie jumped in, hoping to convince her mother of the merit. She handed her the paper cup with her name on it and took a sip of her warm beverage. "With so many papers moving online, it's a real testament to the community that everyone in Harmony Cove still subscribes to the local paper."

"It certainly comes in handy when I need to swat a fly," Sharon said with a polite smile.

Sean swallowed. Hard.

"And of course, we're planning the party," he added, glancing at Annie. "I wanted to run a few things by you, if you have a minute."

"Party?" Sharon perked up at this. Another excuse to frequent Sandra's boutique, no doubt.

"We're having a party to celebrate the anniversary of the paper," Annie said, shooting a look at Sean, hoping that he knew not to say anything more.

"No wonder this is the first I've heard of it," Sharon replied, pursing her lips.

"Sean?" Becky waved him over to the counter. "You're all set. The double shot is on the left."

Annie met her mother's eyes. They both knew who that coffee was for, and it wasn't the man who was now all but running to the counter, away from them. A double shot was Mitch Baker's longstanding order, the one that Sharon always prepared for him on his daily visits to the Sweet Harmony Café.

"You're sure you don't want to come to the party, Mom?" Annie said softly.

For a moment, she thought she saw her mother hesitate, but just as quickly Sharon fluffed her pink-streaked hair and tugged her sweater a little lower at her hips.

"The only family party I'm going to this week is for your cousin Hillary," she said. "Besides, it's not like I was invited!"

"I'm inviting you," Annie said, fighting with herself not to reveal the true reason for the event. She may have told Sean and her sisters about her father's retirement, but it wasn't her place to tell her mother any more than it was her role to try to get her parents back together.

Even if that's exactly what she hoped to do.

"I'm sure it would mean a lot to Dad if you were there," Annie stressed. "And it's your success, too," she added, thinking again of the photo of her father working at the café in his early days as the editor. "You were there for all of it."

Again her mother paused but then shook her head. "I have to get back to the café. Molly is too sweet to bother me, but I'm sure the place is swamped with the lunch crowd. You and Sean go ahead and talk about the plans for the paper's party. I wouldn't want to interrupt anything." With a wink, she plucked the shopping bag from Annie's hand.

"Mom," Annie started to protest, but her mother was already speed-walking to the door, shoulders back, chest...out.

"People will want my chowder," she called over her shoulder. "Even Molly can't make it like I do."

Annie gave a sad smile. It was true, no one could make that chowder the way her mother did, and for that she was grateful.

Besides, she had a feeling that her mother needed to be needed. And that maybe she hadn't felt that way by her husband recently.

Sean and Annie walked down Water Street, turning the first chance they could, subconsciously stumbling down the same dirt path they'd always preferred, toward the harbor.

"Okay, admit it," Annie said beside him, a smile lighting her eyes that pulled at his gut, reminding him of the way she used to look up at him when they shared every joke and secret. Every plan and hope.

"What?" Sean said, feeling jumpy. "Admit what?"

If she was going to mention her mother's sweater, he wasn't sure that he could hide the truth from her—or keep from laughing.

"Did you just tell me you had some party-planning idea to run by me as a way to get us both out of that awkward situation back there?"

Oh. Sean felt the tension leave his shoulders, but not completely. There was still the memory of the looks those women in the coffee shop were giving him, like they were just waiting for him to swoop Annie into his arms and tell her he'd made the biggest mistake of his life by leaving her all those years ago.

And that's exactly what he would do if he thought Annie would be receptive to that sort of thing.

"It seems that Marcy isn't the only one who has notions of us rekindling our romance," Sean said with a mild smile.

"Ah, so you read her column?" Annie laughed. "I'm not sure which part was more exciting, the part about you pulling me into your office, or the speculation of what we were doing behind your closed door."

Sean felt his mouth twitch. "I think my personal favorite was the line about the muffled sounds of pleasure that could be heard by passersby."

Annie stopped walking and gaped at him. "She didn't! I didn't read that part!"

"You must not have read all the way to the bottom, then." Sean laughed. His steps felt lighter, despite the heaviness he still carried from last night's conversation with his father. Being here with Annie, the water in full view, the breeze in his face, and their laughter so easy, like old times. It felt right.

It felt like everything that had been missing.

"I don't mind my mother getting notions, actually," Annie said.

Sean looked at her sharply. "Oh?" He tried to keep the hope out of his voice, but it was still there.

Annie met his gaze. "It means she still believes in true love. In people finding a way back to each other."

Sean knew that she was referring to her parents, of course she was, but still, he couldn't lose the opportunity to keep this conversation going.

"And do you?" he asked, struggling to look at her as they

came to a stop where the path met the sand, both of them in inappropriate shoes for taking the walk much farther in this direction. "Do you believe that it's possible for two people to find a way back to each other?"

Annie's breath seemed heavy as she stared at him, and for a moment, the only sounds that could be heard were of the waves rolling in the distance.

"I didn't used to, but now, I sort of have to, don't I?" she asked. "I mean, now I'm standing on the outside, watching two people who shared so many wonderful moments, an entire life of memories, go their separate ways."

"It's a lot different from this view," Sean admitted. He stared out on to the water, at the vast water, that seemed limitless, like their future once had. "But when you're in it..."

"It's hard not to be exactly where they are," Annie finished.

"Maybe you should remind them of the good times then," Sean said carefully, not wanting to overplay his hand. He knew that Mitch wasn't opening up about his marital problems, and he also knew the reason behind it. It was easier not to think about the things that hurt the most.

"You really think that will work?" Annie turned to search his face.

He stared at her, at the girl he had known since she was small enough to still play on the playground down the shore, where children screeched and laughed now, where he thought their children might someday swing and slide. He wanted to protect her now, just like he had back then, but in both instances, he knew that he couldn't.

That sometimes wanting something wasn't enough.

"It's worth a try," he said, being as honest as he could. "If you love someone, it's worth a try."

And Annie was worth it. She always had been. Always would be.

Ten

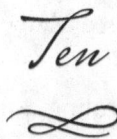

Sean's job was to let everyone at the office know that there was going to be a party on Saturday night—but not the reason behind it. Mitch had yet to announce his retirement, and until he did, Sean could only hope that he would change his mind.

"A party? Why is this the first I'm hearing of it?" Marcy accused, staring at him from behind her smudged glasses.

Sean resisted the urge to offer to buff them on his sleeve.

"Annie and I just came up with the idea this week," Sean explained, immediately wishing he hadn't when Marcy's blue eyes lit up.

"Oh, is *that* what the two of you have been whispering about all week?"

Sean couldn't be sure if Marcy hoped this was the case or would be disappointed if it were. There was no doubt in his mind that she'd been hoping there was something much more personal going on between him and Annie—and that made two of them.

"We've been collaborating on our stories since we're both covering the paper's anniversary. We pooled our research so that we can both make sure our articles are the best they can be."

He could practically see Marcy's imagination taking over as she bobbed her head.

"So you must be spending quite a bit of time together," she said. "Even more than here in the office?"

"Just what we need to do to get the work done," Sean said lightly. Sensing Marcy's frustration, he decided to throw her a bone. After all, she'd likely be his boss come Monday, or at least, his temporary boss. The thought depressed him, not because he didn't like Marcy, but because no one could ever replace Mitch. "It's been nice working with Annie. Like old times."

Marcy's eyes went wide as she chewed the end of her ballpoint pen. "Is it just like old times, Sean?"

Sean shook his head, chuckling softly as he walked away from her desk. Leave it to Aunt Marcy to home in on the heart of the matter. Just like old times, when they'd team up in college on the student paper, which they eventually ran as coeditors. They loved bouncing ideas off each other, working late when it didn't seem like work at all, and ordering cheap takeout when they finally listened to their stomachs.

He thought those days would never end.

Now, he wished he could go back and appreciate each one a little more, knowing that they would.

He refilled his coffee mug before pausing outside Mitch's door, listening for any sound of conversation before tapping on it.

"Come in!" called the friendly voice.

Sean stepped inside the familiar office, with its organized piles that only Mitch understood, the place where he'd spent so much of his pivotal years, learning from the best, and later, longing to be.

His boss in DC was friendly enough, hardworking, and smart as they came, but he wasn't a mentor. Or a friend.

"I wanted to go over some notes on the article with you if you have a few minutes."

"For my best reporter? Of course." Mitch winked, and Sean sank into the visitor's chair, overwhelmed with nostalgia when he realized that the next time he was taking this seat, he might be face-to-face with Marcy and her perpetually dirty glasses. "It seems that you and Annie have been quite busy this week."

"Well, the article is important to us," Sean said. "And so is the paper."

"Which is why you've taken it upon yourself to host a party in its honor." Mitch smiled. "I just got off the phone with my daughter. I'm touched, Sean."

Sean nodded, not wanting to give away the true point of the evening. "Well, working at this paper has been an honor, and a centennial anniversary deserves a celebration."

"And here I thought you and Annie were just exchanging ideas for the article." Mitch grinned. "I should have known that the two of you had other reasons for getting together."

They did, or at least Sean did, not that he'd be admitting as much to Annie or her father. Not when he shouldn't even admit it to himself. Being with Annie was filling a part of his heart that had been empty for so long, but the more time he spent with her, the more he already missed her, now that he knew exactly what her absence felt like.

"Annie and I were going through some old photos, and I found one of you working at Sweet Harmony. She mentioned that you used to work there a lot when you first took over the paper and I thought it might be worth mentioning—or not. Is there anything to that that you'd like to touch upon?" Sean asked, knowing that the subject could be sticky and hoping that he hadn't touched a nerve.

Mitch's face shadowed for a moment as he looked out the window, but when he turned back to Sean, he was smiling, and if Sean didn't know better, he'd say that he saw a shine in the older man's eyes.

"I used to work at the café most days, back when Sharon was just getting the place off the ground. She made that place a second home for our family. For the town, really. Even then, it was always full of people. From day one, it was like the community just chose it as its honorary gathering place. It's home away from home, you could say."

Sean took notes, nodding along. He understood. Sweet Harmony was like that: warm and inviting, the kind of place where you could linger and where you always knew you'd run into a familiar face or two.

"It's always been my mother's favorite spot in town," Sean said, his throat growing tight. He forced his attention on his notepad. He'd covered some of the most devastating events in recent history without getting emotionally invested. Surely, he could do the same now.

"When the café first opened, I'd take my work there every day at lunchtime to get a buzz for new stories by talking to the people, hearing their experiences, and learning what mattered to them." Mitch paused for a moment as his gaze turned wistful. "If there was one place in town with a pulse on the community, it was Sweet Harmony. Still is, I suppose. It's always been important to me to tell the news that people want to hear, not just what I deem worthy. I may be the editor-in-chief, but this paper represents all of Harmony Cove, and I respect that. I hope my predecessor will, too."

Sean held his breath, waiting for it. He knew that this was coming, that Mitch couldn't wait all week without telling the staff about his retirement. And even though Sean had been tipped off, and even though he had braced himself for this conversation, he still wasn't prepared to have it.

A part of him had hoped he wouldn't have to. That Annie had been mistaken. Or that Mitch would change his mind.

But that was like wishing his mother wasn't sick. That his father hadn't pushed him so hard to move all those years ago. That he hadn't left this town and all these people he loved in it, only to return now when it was too late to hold on to them.

When everything had changed.

"There's no easy way to say this, Sean, so I'm just going to come out with it." Mitch pulled in a breath. "I'm letting the staff know individually rather than making a big announcement."

Of course. That was Mitch's way. He was quiet and unassuming. He didn't want a big reaction.

Sean's heart began to pound and he swallowed against the building emotion, wishing he were somewhere, anywhere else, where his feelings were locked up and tucked away.

But they were always here, in Harmony Cove. And now, so was he.

"I've decided to retire," Mitch said with a heavy sigh. "I've already told Annie. And I told Marcy last night. The rest of the staff will learn today. My last edition will be the one-hundredth anniversary. It just seems right."

Right? Sean almost barked out a laugh. It felt wrong. So very wrong.

But this was Mitch Baker. A man he respected immensely. A man who had supported him and whom he would now support in turn.

"Do you have any plans?" he asked, thinking back to what Annie had said about the possibility of Mitch leaving town now that he didn't have a home here in Harmony Cove anymore.

"I have some ideas," Mitch replied without getting into specifics. "Of course, what I've really been focused on is my transition and how this will impact the paper itself."

Of course. Leave it to Mitch to always put the paper first.

Out of both politeness and sadness, Sean said nothing for a moment. They both knew that Marcy couldn't fill her brother's role, not the way he'd handled it, at least. Where he was gentle, she was brash. Where he was a quiet leader, she was a meddler.

Sean supposed that this change would make it easier for him to leave both the paper and Harmony Cove. He knew that he should be grateful for an easy excuse and less regret when he went back to his position in DC. But right now, he just wished that this moment could last a lot longer.

His mind went to his mother. He wished a lot of things could.

"I'm sure there's a lot to consider," Sean said. "But you have a very loyal staff here."

"About that," Mitch said, leaning forward so his elbows rested on his big, messy desk. "I've been wanting to talk to you about the future of this paper."

"Oh, I—"

"I'll get right to the point, Sean. I'd like you to take over the paper."

Sean stared at the man, his mentor, his father figure, and for once in all the years that he'd known him, he was at a loss for words. Of all the things that he'd expected Mitch to say, this was not even in the realm of possibility, not when this was a family paper, and not when he, thanks to his own actions, was not part of the Baker family.

"But—"

Mitch held up a hand. "I know you're here temporarily, but I'm hoping you might consider making it permanent."

Permanent. Nothing in his life felt permanent anymore. Not his family life. Not even his job in DC. But now Mitch was handing him something he'd always wanted—the life he'd always hoped to have, right here in his hometown.

"Doesn't Marcy—"

"Marcy knows about my plan. You have her blessing."

"Marcy knows that you want *me* to take over?" Sean grasped on to the one part of this conversation he could process, a simple fact, one that didn't tap into his emotions or pull him in two directions.

He'd just spoken with her. She'd given absolutely nothing away.

Mitch gave a little smile. "Believe it or not, my sister is an excellent secret keeper when she wants to be. It's why so many still confide in her. She's a good listener, and she cares. And part of caring is knowing when to share something and when to keep it yourself. And I'd like you to keep this to yourself, Sean. For a couple of days, at least. I'd like to be the one to share the news, that is, if you'll accept."

Sean sat in silence, still digesting this information, daring to imagine what it could mean. Staying in town. Not just working at the *Harmony Herald* but running it. Having a say in what stories were told and when.

Following in the footsteps of a man he didn't want to disappoint.

Even if it meant letting down another man—yet again.

"What about Annie?" If he took the job, if he stayed in town, then maybe there would be a chance for them, after all.

"Annie has a big career waiting for her in Seattle," Mitch told him.

Sean knew all about what a so-called big career felt like, and he also knew just how much Harmony Cove meant to Annie. Her family was here. Her friends. All her memories. And the paper. She loved this paper. She was devastated at the thought of her father retiring.

"You're sure that she wouldn't want the job?" Sean wasn't so sure. Annie hadn't dropped any hints about returning to town anytime soon, but she also didn't seem to look very forward to going back to Seattle, either.

Or maybe that was just wishful thinking on his part.

"I've thought about it," Mitch said with a heavy sigh. "But I can't put Annie in that position. If I'd offered her the position, she'd have felt obligated to take it. And the last thing I'd ever want is to have one of my children making important choices about their lives based on what they think will please me."

Someone should try telling his father that, Sean thought bitterly.

"Annie loves this paper, but she's building a name for herself," Mitch said. "She seems so excited about the possibility of her promotion. Who am I to ask her to give that up?"

Sean swallowed a lump in his throat, knowing that he didn't have any more right to ask Annie to stay in town than Mitch did. Less, really.

Knowing that if he took the offer and stayed, something would always still be missing.

"Why me?" Sean finally asked. "I mean, I know I have experience, but—"

"I've had a lot of people pass through these doors," Mitch said. "Reporters come and go. Some see this as a stepping stone, some, like my sister, are content with sticking to one thing."

And some, like Sean, moved on the first chance they had to something more prestigious.

Something better, as Annie liked to say. But it wasn't better. It was just bigger.

"So what do you say?" Mitch asked, his eyes alight with hope.

Sean thought of the conversation he'd had with his father on the deck. And the other one, the morning before he'd left Harmony Cove for good, when he'd made a case for staying put, for making a permanent home in this town.

Nothing he said mattered. His voice might be read by thousands of readers, but it was never heard by the man who needed to listen.

And it never would be, he realized.

"I say that I've never wanted anything more," Sean said, reaching out to take the man's hand.

Except for one thing: Annie.

Annie sat at a window table at Sweet Harmony reading over her notes again, but she couldn't shake the nagging feeling that something was missing from her article. Heart, her editor had said. That's what he wanted to see, something that she hadn't included in her stories in years, something that she still wasn't finding in her words now, try as she might to include it. It was all there: the facts, the history, quotes from the locals who had been reading the paper since her grandfather had run it, or a small but special few like old Eugene Philips, the oldest living resident of Harmony Cove at one hundred seven, who had been just a youngster when her great-grandfather founded it. She'd selected the photos to accompany the article, and even decided on the perfect captions, but something just didn't feel right.

She startled when she sensed someone appear at the table and looked up to see Sean staring down at her, an amused smile on his face.

"This reminds me of all the times I'd find you working in the library back in college," he said as he slid into the chair across from her. "Remember how the one time, I scared you so bad that you screamed out loud?"

Annie laughed. "I nearly got kicked out! I can still remember the glare that the librarian gave me."

"You had to say that you saw a spider," Sean remembered, and for some reason, it touched her that he did.

His dark gaze locked hers as a smile spread across his face, crinkling the corners of his eyes and pulling at her heartstrings. The buzz of the room seemed to grow silent, and for a moment it was just the two of them like it had been all those years ago in their favorite corner of the library.

She snapped her eyes back to her notebook. Right. Back to the article. The entire purpose of this meeting, along with some last-minute party details.

"Did you want to grab something to eat or drink before we start?" she asked, feeling flustered. She saw her mother standing at the counter in the distance, giving her a big thumbs-up behind Sean's back.

Good grief.

"Nah, I had more than enough coffee back at the office," Sean replied, reminding her that this wasn't a personal get-together; there would be no dragging it out. He had a job to get back to, and she had an article to finish.

"I booked Bayview Bistro for the party," Annie told him. At his look of surprise, she said, "On such short notice, I had to pull in some family favors, and luckily my aunt Kathy is more interested in seeing my parents reunite than taking sides."

Molly had taken the liberty of deciding on the menu, and Valerie had discreetly put out feelers for anyone on their invitation list. Aunt Kathy, who would be in charge of the retirement cake, was in a position to let things slip, but Annie knew that she could always count on her.

And on the man sitting across from her right now.

At least, almost always.

"Do you think he'll be pleased?" she asked, worrying that she had blown a possible secret that her father wanted to share.

"I think he might cry," Sean said after a beat, and they both started to laugh. It was no secret that Mitch Baker was a softie, especially when it came to his family and this town. And the paper. The three things he loved most.

Annie's shoulders slumped when she saw her mother pass by again, and she felt her spirit wane.

"He might," she admitted. "He has a big heart. If only my mother could still see it."

"She still won't come to the party?" Sean asked with an apologetic look.

"Nope." Annie had tried asking again just this morning when she'd shown up at the café before the morning rush. "She said that she's going to stay home and have a party for one. Her words." She shook her head.

"Sounds like my life these past few years," Sean said, looking displeased. "Hiding from the people you care about the most doesn't help anyone. Certainly not the one hiding."

Annie looked at him with interest. "And here I thought that you'd be looking forward to getting back to the action after some time in this sleepy little town."

Sean stared out the window on to the street, where passersby leisurely strolled. "It's funny, but being back has only made me miss this town more. When I was away, I tried not to think about it, but now all I want to do is take back the years that I spent somewhere else."

Annie grew quiet. She felt the same way, not that she would let on.

"Maybe I still can." He turned back to lock her eyes.

Annie's entire body stiffened with shock.

"Are you implying that you're planning to stay in Harmony Cove?" She didn't believe it, but the lack of amusement in his face told her that she should.

"I'm not implying it. I'm saying it." Sean's gaze didn't waver as he leaned into the table, so close that she could count his curly eyelashes, feel the heat of his body, and smell the musk of his skin. "I took the long road home, but I don't plan to leave it again."

Annie blinked, trying to digest this information and failing miserably. Sean, who had been so determined to not just leave but stay away, was now back. For good.

"What about your father..." She stared at him, wondering where this certainty had come from, when she knew the pressure that he'd faced all his life.

"A wise person recently reminded me that I wasn't put on this earth only to please my parents, but also to please myself. The truth is that I didn't feel good about the work I was doing for the past few years. I didn't feel proud, and I certainly didn't feel like I was making a difference. My life in Harmony Cove may not be glamorous, and it may never impress my father, but it's an honest life, and I'd like to think that this is what matters most."

Honesty. Annie could only nod because she could hardly say the same for herself. Her entire life back in Seattle was a lie, or at least an exaggeration. She spent her hours fighting loneliness, writing stories on topics that didn't resonate, hoping to make a success of herself. Trying to matter.

But the people she mattered to were here in this town. Her parents, her sisters, her cousins.

And Sean. Who had no intention of leaving Harmony Cove at all.

She forced herself to get back to the article, but even more than earlier, she knew that her heart wasn't in it, that something was missing, something that Sean had found. After all these years.

Six years too late.

"Maybe we should go over the final details for the party," Annie said once they'd exchanged a few last notes for their articles. They hadn't swapped stories like they used to do. She didn't feel proud enough of hers to share it, and she had a sneaking suspicion that Sean wasn't finished with his, either.

"Sure, but then I'd better get back to the desk. This article won't write itself, and you forget, mine is going to print in the Sunday edition," Sean said, confirming her suspicions.

"I would have thought a piece like this would be easy for

you," Annie remarked, hearing the edge in her tone and feeling almost badly about it.

Sean had proven her wrong, after all. Not just by coming back to work at the paper, but by announcing he was staying right here in Harmony Cove.

She'd thought those two things didn't matter to him once. Now she knew that they did.

And that maybe she did, too.

"It's not a puff piece," Sean said, frowning. He studied her for a moment. "As you said, an article like this needs heart. And I think I found the missing piece. Today, in fact."

"Oh?" Annie felt her cheeks burn when their eyes met again, and she wondered what he could mean by that. If it was linked to what was making him stay in town. If it might even have something to do with her.

"Annie," he started and then stopped again.

"Go on," she said, her mouth dry. She didn't know what she wanted him to say, all she knew was that she needed to hear it. There had been years of silence, and like he just said, a lot of time to make up for.

And not many days left to do that.

Sean stared at her for a moment and then shook his head, ever so slightly, as if he'd thought better of what he had been about to say.

"I know you're leaving on Sunday," he said. "But...what do you think about going to that engagement party...together?"

She blinked at him, surprised by the question and, admittedly, pleased. She'd been dreading Hillary and Tim's party all week, but now he was giving her a reason to look forward to it.

"Like...as a buffer?" He knew, after all, how awkward this would be for her.

His expression was unreadable. "Something like that."

Or something more, she wondered. Something like a date.

Her gaze drifted over his face, from his deep, dark eyes that seemed to look right through to the deepest part of her, to the lips that she had kissed a thousand times. She felt a shiver move down her spine.

"It *would* be nice to have a partner in crime," she said slowly. "Seeing as I am attending the engagement party of the man who jilted my sister."

"So it's a date, then?" Sean asked, his smile reaching his eyes.

Annie hesitated, but only for a beat. It was a date.

For better or worse, that's what it was.

And all it ever could be.

Eleven

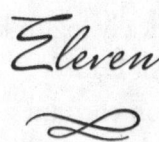

Mornings at the Bayview Bakery were about as common as those spent at the Sweet Harmony Café, and Annie savored the quiet as she sipped her coffee, breathing in the sweet smells wafting from the kitchen.

"What smells so heavenly?" she asked her aunt, who had slipped from the table to carry a tray of breakfast pastries into the lobby of the inn for the weekend guests. Lucy was hard at work in the kitchen, having the time only for a quick greeting when she'd let Annie and Valerie through the door.

"You must be talking about the chocolate croissants," Kathy said. "If you wait around long enough, you can have the first taste."

"Didn't we just eat five slices of cake?" Annie laughed and took another sip of her coffee.

"You've already eaten your dessert, why not go back and have the main course?" Valerie tipped her head.

Annie grinned. "I like the way you think." But then, she'd always appreciated Val's outlook. She took life in stride, which didn't come as naturally for the elder two Baker sisters.

Valerie all but licked her lips. "Fortunately for my waistline, my first walk is in fifteen minutes and this one is a runner. I have to practically jog to keep up with him! Have we decided on a flavor for Dad?"

They had decided on coconut as the official anniversary cake flavor, but they had yet to explain the need for a second cake.

"I think it's all squared away," Kathy said, going back to her coffee.

"Actually," Annie said delicately, glancing at Valerie for approval. "We need a second cake. One just for our dad."

"Oh?" Kathy set down her cup. "That's a nice idea, especially since it is a big day for him. Quite an honor for your entire family. Should we include Marcy's name on the cake, too?"

Perhaps, if Marcy was about to inherit the paper, but Annie couldn't even begin to process that, so she focused on what she knew. The facts.

"We'll keep this to just my father. It's to honor just him. His work and contribution to the community." Annie paused and willed herself not to cry. One look at her aunt and she knew that she just might. She stared at her hands on the table. "He's retiring."

She heard her aunt gasp, and Annie quickly looked up. "Please. Don't say a word. He's going to share it with everyone at the party, I'm sure. The staff will all know by then. The hundredth edition will be his last."

Kathy nodded sadly and then heaved a long sigh. "I

understand. It's...been a big year for Mitch. And for Sharon. For all of you."

That was an understatement.

"Does...your mother know?" Kathy hedged. When Val and Annie shook their heads, Kathy sighed again. "I keep hoping that they'll find a way back to each other."

"That's what everyone used to say about Annie and Sean," Val said, then with a glance in Annie's direction, she said, "No offense, Annie."

"None taken," Annie said mildly as her mind drifted to how she'd left things off with Sean last night...and where the day was yet to lead her.

To Hillary and Tim's engagement party. With Sean.

That would take some explaining so certain family members (make that all family members) didn't misread things.

But would they be so off base? Sean had asked Annie to go to the party with him and she'd accepted. They'd both made a choice.

And this time, Sean was choosing Harmony Cove.

"I'm not sure that anyone ever thought that Caroline and Tim would find their way back to each other," Kathy said, widening her eyes at them both. "But I certainly never thought that Hillary of all people would fall for him!"

Annie couldn't agree more, and Val's pursed lips confirmed her agreement.

"Hillary was there when Tim's brother announced that the wedding was off," Annie said, trying to make sense of it. "She knows what he's like. What he's capable of."

"Maybe he's changed," Val said, though her tone was far from convincing.

"For Hillary's sake, I hope that he has," Kathy said firmly. "And my dear sister is just so excited about this wedding. It's all she can talk about. She's already started making the bridal dress. I think that this event is good for Sandra. It gives her a purpose, and, in a way, a chance to give her daughter the big celebration she never had."

They all knew that Sandra had been married at the town hall in her Sunday church dress, and as someone who prided herself on dressing half the town—and lately her older sister—she more than anyone appreciated a beautiful outfit for a special occasion.

"She always felt badly that she didn't have a dress to pass down to her daughters," Kathy said sadly. "But now she has the chance to make one, and it's even better."

"For Aunt Sandra's sake, I'm glad I'm going tonight, then," Annie said, even as her heart ached for Caroline.

"Do you want me to swing by the house and pick you up or are you getting a ride with Mom and Molly?" Val asked as she stood and stretched her back. The dogs waited for no one.

Annie chewed her lip, knowing that she had no choice but to come clean and brace herself for the inevitable reaction.

"I...sort of told Sean I'd go with him."

Val's eyes widened. "Did you now?" She and Kathy exchanged a giddy wink like two schoolgirls.

"It's not like that!" Annie insisted, even though she wasn't exactly sure if it wasn't exactly what it sounded like.

"Then what is it?" Val's grin was mischievous.

"Just...two old friends," Annie said.

"You and Sean were never just friends," Val pointed out.

True, all true.

"That doesn't mean we can't start now," Annie said. "I don't see a reason to hold a grudge. Not when we've both moved on with our lives."

"Have you though?" Val asked, tipping her head.

Up until this week, Annie thought they had. But now, knowing that Sean planned to stay in Harmony Cove, she wasn't so sure. She might have moved, but had she ever moved on? Or was her heart still stuck in the past, rooted to the one place where she was once happy and maybe still could be?

"I heard you're up for a big promotion in Seattle!" Kathy beamed at her and patted her hand, and even though Annie knew that her aunt was trying to spare her from Val's questioning, she'd only managed to remind her of the promise she'd quietly made to her father.

To do right by him. To make him proud.

And walking away from the opportunity he'd given her, from all that he'd taught her, felt impossible.

"Your father is the most humble man I know, but when it comes to you girls, he can't help but boast," Kathy said fondly.

Annie took another sip of coffee, struggling to swallow it from the lump that had formed in her throat.

"As wonderful as a promotion is, I find your love life far more interesting," Val teased as she gathered her bag.

"Okay, and what about *your* love life?" Annie said, turning the tables.

"I've seen the heartbreak that you and Caroline have suffered," Val said, sobering. "Do you think I'd risk the same for myself?"

Annie was momentarily silenced. Kathy sipped her coffee; if she had an opinion, she withheld sharing it.

"You've dated—"

"Casually," Val said. "And not often."

Annie wanted to encourage her sister to put herself out there, to open her heart to the possibility of love. But she knew that she'd have to do the same for herself, and that it was easier said than done.

Because as much as she wanted to go back to that wonderful time when her heart was full and her future felt bright, she also wanted to avoid the pain that came when it was all suddenly taken away and you were left wondering if any of it was even real.

"Well, much as I'd love to stay, I have a golden retriever to walk who would beg me not to," Val said, moving to the door.

"I'd better get going, too," Annie said with great reluctance. "I still have to find the perfect gift for the bride and groom."

And get ready for another evening with Sean. That was definitely not a date.

Perfect gift aside, by that evening, Annie knew that attending this engagement party was a mistake—one made worse by the fact that she'd agreed to go with Sean.

She stood in front of the full-length mirror that hung on the inside of the closet door in her childhood bedroom, holding up two dresses that Molly had promised her would fit, both of which seemed a little short on the leg and low in the top due to their different builds.

If her mother were around, she'd probably give a firm nod of approval.

"Maybe I should cancel." Annie sighed, turning to hand the dresses back to her sister.

"You can't do that to Hillary!" Molly insisted. "Or me. We can't back out now."

No, they couldn't. It wouldn't be fair to Aunt Sandra.

"But what about Caroline?" Annie reminded her. There was no way that she'd be able to withhold this kind of betrayal the next time they spoke, which was admittedly not very often.

"If you decide to skip it and the rest of us go, it will be even worse!" Molly pointed out. "There's safety in numbers. Then it won't be so...personal."

Annie considered this for a moment and then begrudgingly turned back to the mirror, reconsidering two of the less formfitting dresses.

"Besides," Molly said from where she now sat perched on Annie's bed, "Sean will be very disappointed if you stand him up."

In the reflection, Annie saw Molly's lips curve into a

smile, and she turned to wallop her sister with an old teddy bear.

"It's not like that," she insisted.

Molly just raised an eyebrow and then patted Mr. Bear on the head before setting him back on the faded floral quilt.

"And I wouldn't stand him up," Annie said. "I'd be canceling."

Which was exactly what he'd done to her six years ago, only on a bigger scale. He'd canceled their plans. Their dreams. Their entire future.

"I *should* cancel," she said, reaching for her phone, only to see that Molly beat her to it, snatching it away, behind her back, out of reach. Annie gave her sister a long, patient look. "Aren't you supposed to be the dutiful sister?"

"Is that what I am?" Molly tipped her head in thought. "I suppose I am," she said with a sigh. "Val is more of the rebel, and Caroline is the most serious, and you, well, that one's easy."

Annie was interested in hearing just how her sister defined her. "Do I really want to know?"

Molly smile. "You're the one who aims to please."

Leave it to Molly to pick up on that, Annie thought as she tossed the burgundy dress to the side and began to slip into the navy sheath.

"It's probably why you chose to write the piece for your promotion about the family newspaper," Molly pointed out. "Because you knew that it would make Dad happy."

"I'm writing it because it's newsworthy," Annie told her sister as she struggled with her zipper. "It's inspirational. Not a lot of family papers are around anymore. Papers in general have struggled. It's a real testament to Dad. And to this community."

Which just made his decision to walk away from it all the more bittersweet.

Without being asked, Molly stepped in to help with the zipper. "I know. But I'm just saying, you could have written on any topic, and you chose this one."

"I chose it because I feel connected to it. Because my boss wanted something with heart." Something that she still hadn't managed to put into the article, not without including her own sentimental memories, which would only take away from the authenticity. It wasn't supposed to be an opinion piece, and certainly not a memoir; it was supposed to be about the longevity of a family business and its impact on the community, and about how despite all odds and modernization, traditional values could triumph.

"Speaking of Dad," Molly said, lowering her voice. "Has Mom said anything more about tomorrow night's party?"

Annie swiped on some lipstick and then pulled her hair back into a low bun, the way her mother used to wear hers before she chopped it off and dyed it pink.

"Not to me," Annie said. She looked at Molly hopefully. "Any luck?"

But Molly just shook her head.

"I'm not going to push it," Annie said with a resigned sigh. "It's their relationship, not mine, and what do I know about love?"

"Plenty." Molly dropped onto the bed and picked up one of Annie's old stuffed animals that her mother had held on to all these years. "And certainly more than me."

"You're forgetting that I haven't had a relationship last more than three months since Sean," Annie told her. And she hadn't felt a connection with anyone she'd met since him, either.

"You and Sean were together forever," Molly told her.

"Wrong," Annie said firmly. She walked to her dresser and began filling the gold clutch Molly had lent her with necessities. Once again, she held out her hand for her phone, and this time, Molly obliged. "I *thought* that we'd be together forever. Instead, we were broken up before we were even engaged."

Sure, there might have been a plan for forever, but there had never been a promise.

The doorbell rang, and Annie jumped. Molly just grinned.

"That will be Sean," Molly said, unable to keep the excitement from her voice.

And, despite everything that Annie had just told her sister—and herself—her stomach fluttered with nerves.

"Why don't you ride with us?" she suggested.

A buffer was needed, and Molly would make the perfect chaperone.

"I'm going with Mom," Molly replied with a knowing grin. "Besides, I still have to do my hair."

And before Annie could stop her, she hopped off the bed and darted down the stairs. A moment later, the back door banged shut. Molly hadn't even let Sean inside before hurrying back to the carriage house. She'd decided to leave that honor to Annie.

Annie sighed. Molly might be the mature one of the

Baker clan, but she was still a kid sister, through and through.

Annie walked past her mother's closed door, called out that she was leaving, not that Sharon heard from the noise of the shower, and then hurried down the stairs before she lost her nerve.

"You used the front door," she told Sean when she opened it to greet him.

He was dressed in a gray suit and a light blue tie, and she realized with a start that she hadn't seen him like this since their senior prom, only then he'd worn a rented tux and she'd worn a periwinkle ball gown that Valerie had said made her look like a princess. She'd certainly felt like one. A princess with her prince, on their way to the ball.

And tonight, she felt like that all over again. Sean, all handsome and tall, and her in a dress that Molly had insisted brought out the color of her eyes. They weren't teenagers anymore, and this wasn't their special night, but somehow, with the formality of it, it almost felt like it was.

"I'm not sure about tonight," she admitted, immediately seeing the hurt that passed through Sean's eyes. It was all the reason to have doubts, to stop them from getting too close when it could only end in more heartache.

"We could skip the party," he suggested, giving her a mischievous grin. "Grab a pizza? Head to the beach instead?"

"You mean...play hooky?" It was so tempting, and not just because Annie was dreading the thought of seeing Tim Reynolds again. She longed to be alone with Sean, to pretend for a little while that nothing had changed between them, that their connection was still there, because these past few days, she'd felt it—as strongly as the physical pull that started in her stomach and rose up to her chest every time their eyes met.

His smile was teasing. "Something like that. Sure."

She stared at him for a moment, realizing that he was serious, that he'd do that—for her—and that a part of her wanted just that. The two of them, alone, on the beach, like old times.

But then she thought of what Molly had said, about the family being united on this, and she shook her head.

"We'll go to the party," she said without much enthusiasm.

Sean's expression fell. "Darn. I was sort of hoping you'd say yes."

She would have, she wanted to say. If he'd asked her six years ago—and not about a night on the beach. About a lifetime, together. She'd have said yes if he'd asked.

Instead, she cleared her throat and forced a smile she no longer felt.

"And get our fancy gear all sandy?" She wrapped the silk scarf around her shoulders as she stepped out into the cool spring evening. In the distance, crickets chirped, and she resisted taking Sean's arm the way she might have done, and had done, that glorious night when they were just eighteen, when the summer, and so much more, was within her reach.

"I figured we'd walk," Sean said, doubtfully eyeing her shoes, which were admittedly a little high and already cutting into her heel.

"You're forgetting that I walk in these types of shoes all

the time in Seattle," she told him. "My apartment is ten blocks from the office. I can handle a little walk to the Bayview Inn."

At the mere mention of her life back in Seattle, she felt a sadness wash over her. It was already Friday evening; by this time on Sunday, she'd be on a plane, headed back to the West Coast, to a job she never liked and wasn't even sure she wanted.

Sean must have sensed it, too, because he said, "Seattle must be pretty special to top this."

He held up his arms, embracing the view around them as they approached Water Street. Annie slowed her step to take in all of Harmony Cove, from its shingled homes and flowering gardens to the cobblestoned road flanked with storefronts owned and operated by people she'd known all her life. The town was quiet now, but somehow it had never felt more alive to her knowing that everything—and everyone—she had ever loved was all tucked neatly inside it.

"Nothing can top this," she said with a lump in her throat. Nothing ever could.

Sean stood in a corner of the bistro, which had been transformed for the occasion with white tablecloths, clusters of candles, and pastel flower arrangements, nursing his beer and watching Annie congratulate the happy couple—who did seem happy. Despite the complicated history, there was a large turnout for the celebration, nearly as big as the one expected for tomorrow night in this very venue, and he hoped that it would be just as joyous, even if his own feelings were mixed about it.

He knew what Mitch had told him about wanting to announce his retirement plan tomorrow, but Sean didn't feel right not letting Annie know that he was going to be taking over the paper. She'd trusted him with the news of her father's retirement, and withholding this development from her left him with a secret he didn't want to keep.

He frowned into his beer before taking another sip, nearly choking when Travis came up behind him and gave him a hard slap on the back.

"Why so serious?" his cousin chided. "Last I checked, this was a party."

It was a party all right, down to the balloons and streamers and the floral centerpieces that anchored all the tables. People were already dancing at the far end of the room, and champagne was flowing.

And all Sean could think about was how much he'd rather be on the beach with a pizza. And Annie.

"I saw you walk in with Annie." Travis smirked. "Marcy saw, too."

Sean could only shake his head. Of course she did. But what Marcy saw and what Marcy chose to report were not his concern. Sure, come next week, he could edit her column, but Sean wasn't looking to put his name on the paper. He was hoping to carry the torch.

He was finally an official part of the Baker family, even if it wasn't in the way he'd ever hoped to be.

"And who are you here with tonight?" Sean asked his cousin, knowing the answer. Travis had come alone, hoping an engagement party would offer an opportunity to meet a fresh face.

"Oh, a few ladies have caught my eye." Travis sipped his beer and cast his gaze over the room.

"Haven't you known most of these women since kindergarten?" Sean replied with a laugh.

"Not the friends of the family," Travis said with a grin. "There are a few out-of-towners here today. And I thought I'd show one or two of them their way around town this weekend."

"Doesn't it get old after a while?" Sean asked him, feeling exhausted just listening to Travis.

Travis looked at him like he was crazy. "Talk to me when I'm forty. I'm having fun, cousin. You should do the same."

Fun. That was something that Sean hadn't had in a long time. Lately, though, this past week, he had laughed and smiled, and felt lighter than he had in years.

He looked across the room, searching through the crowd until his eyes came to rest on Annie. His gut tightened and he took a sip of his drink. Good things didn't last in his world.

"You mean to tell me that in all these years you've been away you didn't casually date?" Travis challenged him.

"Not by choice," Sean replied tightly. Nothing about his last six years was by choice, even if he had ultimately been the one who made it. "A few casual dinners here and there, but nothing that amounted to anything. You know me, I'm a one-girl type of guy."

"One girl specifically," Travis replied, his gaze shifting across the room. "Have you told her yet?"

Sean looked at his cousin sharply. They both knew who Travis was referring to. "Told her what?"

"Come on, Sean." Travis leveled with him. "We both know you still love her."

Sean couldn't argue with that if he tried. "Not sure it matters. She's heading back to Seattle on Sunday."

"Ever think that maybe she'd stay if she had a good enough reason to?" Travis asked before walking away, smoothly joining a group of women that Sean had never seen before, who seemed more than happy to welcome him into their fold.

Sean sipped his drink, remembering Mitch's words, his concern for pressuring Annie to move back to town, to keep her here against her wishes.

But a job and a life were two very different things, and he was proof of that. And maybe, if the paper couldn't bring Annie back to Harmony Cove for good, then something else might.

Something a little more personal.

Annie had to admit that Hillary and Tim seemed happy together. But then, so had Caroline and Tim.

And her mom and dad.

And she and Sean.

Annie caught his eye across the room as the speeches were finishing up—one from Lucas Reynolds, which was stilted and brief, and another more emotional, tearful, and rambling effort from the bride-to-be's mother. Sandra had waited a long time to plan a wedding for one of her daughters and she'd already told everyone who would listen tonight about the dresses she was making for the entire bridal party. The Bayview Bistro was full of familiar faces, and lots of people who wanted to know all about Annie's life in Seattle, the big promotion that was in the works, and of course the *Herald*'s centennial anniversary.

There were more than a few suggestive glances at Sean—and her mother, who was wearing the magenta dress that Aunt Sandra had hand-selected for her, right down to the over-the-top necklace.

But now Annie had been standing on her feet for two hours, her heels hurt, her legs were cramped, and she was all talked out. Long ago, after a busy day like this, she'd have wanted nothing more than to fall back into the quiet, easy company of a man who was now giving her a conspiratorial grin a few feet away.

He *was* her so-called date for the night. She supposed that it wouldn't hurt to pay him a *little* attention, even as she felt the attention of half the crowd drift from her cousin Hillary to her as she moved to the back of the room.

"Wishing we'd ditched this for the pizza yet?" Sean whispered when she came to stand beside him.

She snorted, then covered her mouth, fighting off her laughter as Sandra tearfully raised another glass to her firstborn.

Annie and Sean did the same, and Annie found herself getting a little teary herself when she saw Hillary lean in for a swoony kiss with her fiancé, not out of sympathy for her sister, who would probably faint if she were here tonight, but because Hillary and Tim looked so in love, so besotted, so certain of their future together. So hopeful.

She knew that look, that feeling of only ever wanting to be with one special person.

And the heartache when you knew that you couldn't.

That you'd never feel their hands on your skin again, or their lips on your mouth, or hear their voice deep into the night, when the rest of the world was asleep.

"Weddings," she said, fanning her eyes. She took a sip of her champagne, now warm from chatting all night, to cover her embarrassment. Without discussing it, they moved out of the bistro and into the lobby of the inn, where the cluster of sofas and chairs surrounding the blazing fireplace was empty.

She sank into the nearest couch, and Sean joined her, sitting close, warming her nearly as much as the crackling flames.

"Do you think you'll come back for the big day?" Sean asked.

Annie hadn't considered this, and not only out of loyalty to her sister. She usually only visited Harmony Cove once a year, less even, as Valerie had pointed out. And if she got the big promotion, she probably wouldn't have a vacation day for a while.

"Work is an easy excuse," she said, shaking her head. "Caroline is the real reason."

"Darn," Sean said, the disappointment obvious in his deep voice. "I was hoping we might go together."

Annie's heart skipped a beat and she had to look away from his handsome face to fight her own disappointment. It might have been nice to spend more time with Sean, but that, like Caroline and Tim, simply wasn't meant to be.

Their chance had come and gone years ago, and now they had made new lives for themselves.

She just never thought that Sean would have chosen to make one here on the Cape. Looking at him now, she still didn't believe it. He might say it, but she was yet to see a reason for why he'd stick to it.

"I'm sure there will be plenty of people you know at the wedding," Annie remarked, then, her chest tightening when she thought of the room full of attractive women that Hillary knew from her college days, she added, "And some you don't."

"Is it strange to admit that I've never been to a wedding before?" Sean mused.

Annie struggled to believe that. She had been to at least three, maybe four weddings over the years, two of college friends who were surprised when she showed up without Sean, and the rest coworkers in Seattle.

"How did you manage that? Do I need to remind you that we're in our thirties?"

"Like I said, it's been all work these past few years," Sean said with a shrug. "I basically live out of a suitcase. I'm not exactly in one place long enough to make friends."

It was only then that Annie realized just how lonely Sean's life had become. That maybe it was as empty as her own.

She took another sip of her drink and then, remembering that it was warm, set it down on the end table.

"I think I've had enough of all this wedding talk," she

said, the irony not lost on her that weddings were a popular subject of her column. For now.

The thought that it all might change had filled her with a sense of hope for a while, but since returning to Harmony Cove, she no longer felt so optimistic. She'd lost her touch, her ability to get to the heart of a story, and wasn't that the *Herald*'s very tagline? The one that her father prided himself on, the one that he had drilled into her from a young age?

Being back here was supposed to cure her, but instead, she feared that she'd leave feeling even worse than before she arrived.

"Do you ever wonder—" Sean started, and then stopped.

"Go on," she pressed as her heart began to speed up. Even though the lobby was quiet, noise drifted in from the party in the bistro, the din of conversation loud over the music, and she had to lean in to be sure she would hear him. She could feel the warmth of his body, his breath tickling her neck, and she pressed a little closer as the music changed to one of those cheesy line dance songs and a cheer went up in the other room. It seemed that everyone wanted to be a part of it.

But not her. Because all she wanted was right here. In this town. Her family. Her friends. Her home.

And this man.

"Do you ever wonder what our wedding might have been like?" he asked.

She stared at him for a moment, her voice caught in her throat, but then anger coursed through her. "We were never engaged."

"You know I wanted to ask you." His voice was nearly

lost in the shift in volume, making her wonder if she'd just imagined it.

But his eyes were dark and intense, and he was staring at her, waiting for her to answer.

"But you didn't," she said simply. And darn if that didn't still hurt, even now.

She'd expected it that summer he finished grad school. Instead, she'd been handed other life-changing news.

"We were going to take on this town together," she reminded him. "This was our home. It's where we always came back to in the end."

"And I did," Sean said. "I mean it, Annie, I'm not going anywhere this time. I'm here for good."

"But why, Sean? I wasn't enough to keep you here, but now something else is?" She shook her head. "I didn't mean it that way. Your mother…"

"She doesn't have much time," Sean said, and they both grew silent at that. "But I do. Or maybe I don't. Look, being back here has made me realize just how much time has passed. How much I've lost. Nothing I've done for the past six years is half as important as anything that was waiting for me right here in Harmony Cove. I don't want to lose one more day."

It would be so easy to harden her heart to his words or to choose not to believe them. But she knew that he was telling the truth, that he meant it because she felt the same way. She'd left this town and didn't know if and when she would be back, but that didn't mean that her heart wasn't in it. That it always had been.

Maybe his had, too.

They were sitting close, nose to nose, so close that she could see the flecks of gold around his pupils, and before she could say anything more, move away, or make an excuse to leave, she felt his hand on her waist, pulling her close, and he was leaning in, his lips so close to hers, they were almost touching, but not quite. It was as if he, too, was savoring this moment, one that they'd never thought they'd get back, one that they thought was lost forever.

His mouth found hers, soft and familiar. His hands were warm on her bare back, pressing her tight against his chest as their kiss deepened, and as much as every part of her wanted to push him away, the bigger part of her wanted to sink in, relax, and let herself fall. His taste was as familiar as his touch, and she kissed him back, slowly at first, and then with more need.

To make this kiss matter. To make it last.

If not for forever, then somehow, for a lifetime.

Twelve

The kiss was not front-page news, but that was only because the Harmony Happenings column was buried on page nine, much to Marcy's endless dismay.

"I still don't understand how you found out!" Annie tossed the paper onto the table she'd been decorating for tonight's event and leveled a hard stare at her aunt. "You weren't even at the engagement party last night!"

"Wasn't I?" Marcy blinked slowly. "I wasn't *invited*. There's a difference, dear. And you're forgetting that the inn is a public place, and the lobby is in full view of town, especially when it's all lit up inside."

Annie was only aware that she was gaping at her aunt when she caught Sean's grin from across the room. Since the bistro wasn't open for lunch service, Aunt Kathy had given them early access to set up for the party tonight, and it had seemed fitting that Annie, Sean, Marcy, Molly, and Val would pitch in, but Annie was regretting this decision immensely.

Val couldn't stop grinning more than a little mischievously as she taped balloons to the corners of the doorways, and Molly looked as starry-eyed as Marcy probably expected Annie to be—only Annie couldn't focus on the kiss, however wonderful it might have been, because she was too busy worrying about the entire town knowing.

And about leaving. Tomorrow.

The thought landed like a rock in her stomach, and nothing she did or said would make it go away. With each streamer she hung, and every glance at Sean, her heart felt a little heavier. Her father was retiring. The paper would no longer be his. She had to make him proud.

Even if it made her miserable.

Molly was right. She did aim to please. Because the thought of not making her father happy was even worse than the thought of him putting his final edition of the paper to bed tonight.

"Think of it this way," Sean said once Marcy had moved on to the floral arrangements—simple but colorful seasonal arrangements that were a sharp contrast to last night's elegant and romantic ambiance. "Our kiss took the spotlight away from Tim and Hillary's engagement party, which was probably for the best if Caroline reads the column."

"True," Annie said begrudgingly. "That was *one* good thing to come from it."

"The only good thing?" Sean's gaze was hopeful, and Annie fell silent for a moment, wishing that she could tell him—and herself—what she wanted, but knowing that she couldn't.

"I don't appreciate Marcy's wording," she said, dodging

his question. She picked up the paper again and tapped on the article. "'A rapturous public display of unbridled passion!'"

Sean was grinning. "Well. Wasn't it?"

Annie firmed her mouth against a laugh. "You're incorrigible."

"And that's why you love me," he joked.

They both fell silent, as if Sean realized he had crossed a line—or hit a nerve.

But the truth of the matter was that Annie did still love him. She'd felt it last night, with their kiss, and she'd known it long before then. She'd never really stopped.

True love didn't stop. And maybe it didn't end.

And where did that leave her? she wondered. Other than on a flight back to Seattle tomorrow.

At six o'clock that evening, Annie finished brushing her hair and zipping her dress and looked at the unfinished article on her open laptop. The word count was there, along with the photos and anecdotes, the history dating back to her great-grandfather, who had been raised by a fisherman and a schoolteacher, but Annie couldn't help but feel that something was still missing, and she could only hope that if there was ever a night to find it, it would be tonight.

Time had run out. For the article. For her dad's time at the paper.

And, much as she hated to think about it, for her and Sean.

Grabbing her evening bag, Annie stepped into the hall and paused outside of the bedroom door across from the staircase. It wasn't too late for her mother to join them, but she'd pushed the topic enough, and it was her father who had taught her at an early age when she was running her middle-school newspaper that sometimes you had to know when to let something go. If someone didn't want to talk, then they wouldn't.

Still, Annie needed to try.

"Mom?" Through the closed door, she heard a rustling of fabric, and then what sounded like her mother blowing her nose. "We're heading out. We can wait for you if you want to join us."

Another sniff, louder this time. "I told you I'll be just fine here tonight. I need to weed my garden, anyway."

Annie felt a smile tug at her chest. Her mother was never one to sit idle, much like the rest of the Baker clan. The café had closed hours ago, but instead of relaxing in a hot bath or on the porch with a glass of wine, Sharon was already thinking of how to keep busy.

It made Annie's mind drift to her father, and how he planned to spend his retirement. She knew that he wouldn't have the time to sit on the beach for more than a few hours, regardless of how much he appreciated the coastline and views. He was a man who was always engaged, always active.

Meaning, he must have a plan. And she intended to find out what it was.

Knowing that her mother wasn't going to change her mind about tonight's party, Annie sighed. "Well, you know where to find us."

"Thanks, honey," her mother's voice came, hollow and distant through the door, "but I won't."

Annie felt a surge of disappointment and frustration. "Well, if you do, we'll all be there, and we'd love to have you. Think of it as an excuse to wear one of those cute new outfits that you bought at Sandra's shop."

She must be even more desperate than she'd thought, considering that those clothes were better marketed to a teenage clientele. And if she thought that giving her father a retirement party was a surprise, then seeing his wife in her new look would probably send him into shock.

Her mother didn't reply, but Annie waited a beat just in case. Again she heard her mother blow her nose, and if she didn't know better, she might think that her mother was crying.

"Mom? Everything okay?"

"Just allergies," her mother replied in a strained voice. "You know how I get them every spring. Don't worry about me. You girls go and have fun."

So that was it, then. She'd tried her best. But as Annie walked down the stairs and into the kitchen, where Molly was waiting, she couldn't help but think that she'd let everyone down.

Especially herself.

"No luck?" Molly asked, and Annie shook her head.

"Dad's waiting," Annie said, checking the old clock that hung on the wall in the front hallway. When the girls were little and had to sit on the steps for time-out, they used to watch it slowly tick away the minutes until they could go back to their fun. Now Annie watched it slowly move her closer to the time when she had to go back to Seattle. And whatever was waiting for her there, which didn't feel like much, even with a possible promotion. "We should go."

They headed out together as far as the town, and then Annie went to the newspaper office while Molly headed to the restaurant to be sure everyone had arrived. A little fission of excitement shot through Annie's stomach at the thought of it, and she hurried to her father's office, eager to get the night started.

But when she got to her father's office, she saw that he was sitting in the dark, only the glow of his computer screen lighting the room.

"Dad?" Annie flicked on the light, relieved to see that he was dressed to go out in a button-down shirt and slacks, but the pensive look on his face was troublesome. "How long have you been sitting in the dark?"

Her father chuckled. "You know me. I got lost in a story. Couldn't stop to stand and turn on a light." He grew quiet for a moment as his gaze went back to the screen. "Hard to believe it's my last one before I put this puppy to bed."

"Dad." Annie felt her voice break and she dropped into the visitor's chair. "You know that you can still change your mind. It's your paper. You don't have to retire. Not today, anyway."

Mitch's eyes were gentle when he looked at her, nodding along, and for a moment she thought that he might agree with her. Instead, he gave her a wan smile and said, "Change is never easy, but sometimes it is necessary. I've had a good run here, but it's time for the next chapter."

"Do you...know what you plan to do next?" She held her breath while she waited for the answer.

"I do," he said with a smile that reached his eyes.

Annie was slightly surprised by this, even though she knew she shouldn't be. This was her father. A man who always knew what tomorrow held, whose life up until this day meant coming to this paper, and putting in a hard day's work. But his life had been uprooted lately, and maybe that had brought along further reflection and change.

Either way, he seemed strangely happy if the gleam in his eyes said anything.

"I'm happy for you, Dad."

Just like with her mother, Annie knew better than to push. Instead, she cleared her throat, fought back the burn in her chest, and reached across her father's desk for the last time to shake his hand, just like he'd done four years ago, when she'd accepted the job offer in Seattle, only that time, it was he who was reaching across the desk, a silent gesture to tell her that he understood, that she had his support, that she was on the right path.

Oh, Dad.

Why did it feel just as wrong today as it had then?

Not releasing her hand, Mitch instead clasped it with his other hand and stood, coming around the desk, and pausing only to turn and look at the room for a long, quiet moment.

"We did good work here," he said.

"*You* did good work here," she told him. "I'm proud of you, Dad."

"Not as proud as I am of you, sweetheart," he said, his eyes glistening.

Annie felt a single tear trickle down her cheek and then she watched as her father turned off the light. The glow from the screen remained, the final edition off to print. And even though Annie knew the paper would continue and remain in the family, and that her father was embarking on a new phase that he was looking forward to, she couldn't help but feel for the second time in her life like one of the best chapters in her life had come to an end.

If Mitch was surprised by the turnout for the party, he did a good job of hiding it. The only thing that might have stunned him more was if Marcy had burst from the cake—or maybe Sharon, in one of her new pink outfits.

But Annie's mother was a no-show, despite the last bit of hope that Annie had clung to. She'd searched the crowd for her as soon as they'd walked into the restaurant, and she'd seen her father do the same, his smile slipping for a telling second before lifting again as he greeted each of his guests—which felt like it amounted to the entire town.

Annie helped herself to a slice of coconut cake, her father's favorite flavor, and then wandered over to Sean, who seemed as overwhelmed by the night as she was.

"We pulled it off," he said, seeming both surprised and exhausted.

Annie realized that she felt the same way. "Almost. There's still the big retirement celebration." She checked her watch, deciding to give it a little more time. "We always made a good team. Thanks for doing this. It means the world to my dad."

They fell silent for a moment as they watched Mitch across the room, for once not brushing away the attention but allowing himself to be honored the way he so rightfully deserved.

"You're dressed up," Annie remarked when she turned back to Sean, motioning to his tie and sport coat. *And handsome*, she didn't add, but oh, did she think it.

"It's a big night," Sean replied with a shrug.

For the family, Annie thought but didn't say. Sean had managed to convince her this week that he did care about the paper, this town, her family—and her. He of all people knew what this newspaper meant to Mitch and her; he had worked tirelessly by their sides summer after summer, learning the craft and mastering it well.

"I'm sure it meant a lot to him that he got to work with you one last time," Annie told Sean, even as the hurt lodged tight in her stomach, reminding her that she'd had that chance, too, but only for this week. "You made my father proud."

His expression shifted, betraying his inner emotions, and Annie was moved to see just how much this meant to him. And it pained her to think of how he'd never felt that with his own father and maybe never would.

All the more reason to make things work in Seattle, Annie told herself. She had made her father proud, and she'd basked in that, and it had kept her going all these lonely, soulless years when she yearned for home and her family and even the man who was standing before her right now.

The man who had broken her heart. And might again if she gave him the chance.

"Not as proud as you make him," Sean said. His gaze held hers for a moment before he cleared his throat. "It's... been nice. Working together again this past week."

It had been. And now, tonight, it was officially over. Sean's article had gone to print. Hers would be handed in tomorrow. And then she'd be on a plane to Seattle.

While Sean stayed behind.

"I always loved working together," Sean went on.

A lump rose in Annie's throat. She could only manage a nod.

"And...I've always loved you, Annie." His dark eyes were unwavering, and Annie stared at him, barely breathing, her mind spinning, wanting to say something in return and not even knowing where to begin.

It would be so easy to tell him the truth—that she'd always loved him, too, that she'd never stopped, even when she wanted to, even when she'd tried to run from it.

"Distance doesn't change feelings," he said softly.

Her eyes prickled with tears. "No," she said, knowing just how true it was. "Sometimes it makes them stronger."

His mouth quirked, and he took a step toward her. "I know I can't ask you to stay, but...I wish you would consider it, Annie. This is your home. Your family."

She felt a moment of hope fill her chest, a flicker of a life that was exactly as she'd once imagined it would be. One spent here, in Harmony Cove, with the people she loved most. Her sisters. Her mother. Sean.

Her father.

She glanced across the room to where her dad now stood, chatting with his friends. When he felt her stare on him, he glanced over and gave her a wink, and just like that, the perfect image burst.

She could stay. Give up the job in Seattle, maybe even come back and start working for the paper again. But she'd be working for Marcy, not her father. And even though Sean was saying everything that she wanted to hear, he'd said it once before, too.

And he'd still left. This town. The paper. And her.

"Everything has changed," she said, feeling the weight of her words in her chest.

"It doesn't have to be for the worse," Sean pressed, setting a hand on her arm.

It was warm and heavy and she wanted to shake it off as much as she wanted him to keep it there. Just as quickly, he dropped it, leaving her alone, reminding her that so much recent change had been for the worse. Her parents were splitting up. Her father was leaving the paper. Sean's mother was dying.

"How can you be so sure?" she asked, her voice barely above a whisper.

Sean stared at her with a deep frown, wrestling with whatever it was he wasn't sure he could tell her, but then let out a long sigh when Marcy began tapping her fork against her wineglass with enough force to break it, silencing the room.

Frustrated, Annie watched as her aunt moved to the back of the room, where she raised her glass in a toast.

"Now you all know how I feel about public speaking,"

she said, and everyone laughed. Marcy preferred to be on the listening end. "But this is a special occasion, not just for my family, who is here tonight, but for the *Harmony Herald*, which wouldn't exist without the support of this amazing community. More than anything, this night is about my brother, Mitch, who took this paper into the twenty-first century and made our father and grandfather proud. I know our dad is up there looking down on us right now, and I know that he couldn't have asked for more. Well done, Mitch. Well done."

Tears brimmed in Annie's eyes and she quickly wiped them away as they started to fall, hot and fast. She didn't dare look at Sean, because she could sense by his stillness beside her that he felt all the emotions, too. That he'd never have the feeling of knowing he made his father proud. That it was the end of an era, one that she foolishly thought would never end.

But all things eventually did, didn't they?

She watched through blurred vision as her father humbly walked to the front of the room, pausing here and there to receive a pat on the back, or give a handshake, his smile bashful. He stopped to collect himself when he took Marcy's place, giving Molly a little wave over in the far corner, and then Valerie, standing near the cousins. When he craned his neck to spot Annie, he winked at her, and it was that one gesture, one of simple reassurance, that reminded her that they were connected at this moment, that he understood, and that somehow, it would all be all right.

People changed, like he'd told her that first day back in the office. And this week was proof of that. But deep down, in their heart of hearts, where it mattered most, they were still the same. Under all that pink, her mother was still at the helm of the family nest, tending to her garden and nourishing the town. And even though Annie's father would no longer be the voice of the community, he would always be her dad.

Mitch paused for a moment, his eyes scanning the room before he pulled in a breath and looked down. He nodded his head once, and Annie knew that his decision had been made. He hadn't made it lightly, and this couldn't be easy, but he was determined. He always had been.

"As you all know, you're gathered here tonight to celebrate the hundredth anniversary of our community's paper. Sometimes, I feel like I've been running the paper for a hundred years, or at least working for it."

The audience chuckled but quickly died down. They could sense something was coming, and there was a shift, people stopped sipping their wine, their conversations forgotten.

"With luck and hard work, it's my hope that the paper will go on for another hundred years," Mitch continued. From across the crowd, he met Annie's eyes. "But I will not. To everything, there is a season, and I have had mine, and what a remarkable journey it has been. And I can think of no better time to take my exit than tonight, after putting the hundredth-anniversary edition to print."

A gasp went up in the room, and eyes darted, people whispering in disbelief and confusion. Only those in the know remained silent. Annie drew a heavy sigh.

"I've been thinking about this for a while, but the truth

is that I couldn't leave without knowing that I had someone to fill my seat. Someone who loves this paper and this town as much as I do. Someone with the vision to maintain its integrity, and to be committed to this community." Mitch looked to the back of the room again, and Annie felt the crowd go still.

He couldn't mean—he didn't mean—but Seattle... He'd pushed for it. Encouraged her to go! He'd been so proud when she'd gotten the job! Told her it was a bigger opportunity than she could have ever had here. He seemed to live vicariously through her. Her success was his success. She'd done right by him.

"And then something unexpected happened," Mitch went on. "And someone returned to town, just when I needed them. Just when maybe they needed me. And us. All of us."

Annie's heart was positively pounding now. This party was supposed to be his surprise, not hers. She felt like the air was locked in her chest and she couldn't breathe. Her entire body was shaking at the enormity of what her father was about to say, and she couldn't even trust her knees to carry her to the back of the room to accept what he was suggesting.

It all made sense now, why he had decided to walk away just when she returned, at a crossroads in her career, just before a promotion made it more difficult to walk away. She should have known that he understood, just like he always did, that as much as she needed to get away from Harmony Cove four years ago, it was finally, at long last, time for her to come home.

She stared at her father as time seemed to go still, and he grinned at her, setting a hand to his chest, just like he always did when he wanted to show her he was proud. She smiled through her tears, nodding, telling him that yes, she would take over the paper, she'd carry on the legacy, that this was the role he'd groomed her for all along.

He gave her a long, tender look that was filled with more pride than she'd seen even when she told him about being up for a promotion. A look that filled Annie's lungs with air and made her breathe easily for the first time in longer than she could remember. The ache in her chest that she'd learned to live with was finally gone, replaced with hope, and excitement for the future that she hadn't had since she and Sean were both working at the *Herald*, thinking about what the years ahead might hold for them.

Her father gave her another wink, and then his gaze drifted to her right. To the man standing beside her.

"Sean Morrison," her father said loudly. "Will you come up here so that I can introduce the new editor-in-chief of the *Harmony Herald*?"

Annie felt the blood drain from her face as she turned to stare at Sean. He was looking at her with a tense jaw, his eyes dark with understanding when they met hers.

"You?" she could barely whisper.

"Annie." His voice was strangled. "I wanted to tell you, but your father—"

"You *knew*?" The tears came hard and fast and she quickly blinked them away before they could fall. People were clapping; the room was loud and celebratory. One of Harmony Cove's own had returned.

But it hadn't been her.

She knew her father was happy with his decision, that people were expecting a speech, and that Sean was waiting for her approval. But she didn't care.

All she cared about was that her heart felt like it was breaking in two. That once again, the man she'd trusted, cared about and dared to love, had let her down.

In the worst possible way.

The light was on in the kitchen when Annie stepped inside the house a short time later, feeling like a hundred hours had elapsed since she'd left. Her feet ached nearly as much as her heart, and she slipped off her shoes and padded to the back of the house, where her mother was standing at the big kitchen island, scooping homemade ice cream into a bowl.

Her face was washed clean of the garish makeup, her hair pulled back, and her tattered floral robe tied at her waist. For the first time since returning home, Annie's mother looked like, well, her mother.

"Want some?" she asked, holding up the cardboard container.

Annie inspected the handwritten label: blackberry cream. She settled onto a counter stool while her mother prepared a bowl for her and then stowed the container in the freezer along with a dozen others that she prepared in her free time. Ice cream making was a hobby of hers, though she did keep vanilla on hand at the café to accompany her pies.

"How was the party?" her mother asked after they'd each taken a few bites.

Annie didn't know how to respond to that question, and not for the reasons she would have cited earlier that evening.

"Do you want the truth?" she asked.

Her mother looked at her with interest, then nodded.

"It was terrible." Annie burst into tears.

Alarmed, her mother set down her spoon and pulled Annie in for a long, tight embrace. Stroking her hair, she let her cry it out, just like she had as a child until Annie finally pulled back.

She didn't ask what had happened but waited patiently for Annie to explain when she was ready.

"Dad retired from the paper," Annie blurted. She knew that her mother would hear it by tomorrow, anyway, when the paper hit everyone's front steps.

If Sharon was surprised by this, she didn't show it. Instead, she nodded slowly and then let out a long breath. "Something tells me that isn't what has you this upset."

"Sean is taking over as editor of the paper," Annie said. "Sean!"

Her mother's eyebrows shot up, but then she sighed. "Sean loved that paper as much as you did, Annie."

"Do," Annie insisted. "I still love that paper. It's because of the *Herald* that I became a journalist."

Her mother tipped her head. "Did you ever think that it's because of your father that you chose your career?"

Annie blinked, surprised to hear her mother even mention him. "Of course. I mean, Dad taught me everything he knows."

"It wasn't just about learning the business, Annie." Her mother's smile was fond. "You were always a Daddy's girl, always content to just sit by his side, even on that old porch swing. It wouldn't have mattered if your father was running a paper or fishing for lobster."

Annie's eyes burned with tears. "But I left."

Her mother opened her palms. "Leaving someone doesn't always mean we stop loving them."

Annie brushed a tear from her cheek, daring to wonder if her mother was referencing herself.

"Do you...still love Dad?" Her heart began to pound as she waited for the response.

When her mother slowly nodded, the tears fell harder. "You know he loves you, too, Mom. He loves this family."

"I know," her mother said with a sigh. "I know. But somewhere along the way, he got lost in that paper. He spent more and more hours there, and some days it felt like it would only ever be that way."

Except now. He'd retired.

Annie didn't say it because she knew that they were both thinking it, and the sadness in her mother's eyes told her that instead of being happy about the decision, Sharon was as worried as Annie was.

"What's he going to do without the paper?" Annie wondered aloud. "And without you?"

"Probably the same thing that I've been doing without him," her mother replied with a heavy sigh.

Annie gave her mother a pointed look. "You mean, going out to bars and trying out a new look?"

A small smile lifted the corners of her mother's mouth. "I stepped out of my comfort zone. I thought that if I did, something would change. But I hated being dragged to all those bars by my sister when all I really wanted to do was curl up next to the fireplace with a hot cup of tea. And I didn't like chatting with other men or wearing clothes that made people look at me. The only person I ever wanted to notice me was your father. I guess I thought if I did something drastic, he finally would."

"Oh, Mom." Annie's voice broke as she reached out to take her mother's hand.

"I guess I was trying to figure out who I was," her mother said, giving a sheepish grin, "if I wasn't Mitch's wife. But running from myself wasn't the answer."

Running from the people you loved, or where you were most yourself, never was, Annie thought grimly.

"Can I make a confession?" her mother whispered.

Annie braced herself. She wasn't sure she was ready for any more surprises.

"I sort of like the pink highlights," her mother said.

Annie stared at her mother for a moment, studying her face, the fine wrinkles around her soft green eyes, the highlights that did somehow suit her free spirit.

"You know what? I do, too," she said, and with that, they both burst out laughing.

"I don't know what I'll tell poor Sandra when I hand off my new wardrobe," Sharon said when they finally settled down, wiping the tears from their eyes, some of amusement, some not so much.

"I'm sure she'll be disappointed to lose her best

customer," Annie agreed. She eyed her mother hesitantly. "And her sidekick. Unless...you plan to keep dating?"

Her mother took a breath and then shook her head. "I never liked spending my nights out on the town. I only did it because it was better than sitting in this house all alone, remembering the days when it used to be filled with four little girls, and..."

Her voice trailed off, and she turned to face the window.

"Molly is just out back," Annie urged. "And...I'll visit more."

But it would just be a visit. And the thought of returning to Seattle tomorrow gave her a stomachache.

It wasn't where she wanted to be, and it certainly wasn't where she wanted to stay. And much like her mother's reasons for joining her sister at the local watering holes, she was only going back to the West Coast because it beat staying in Harmony Cove, remembering all that she once had...and had lost.

Thirteen

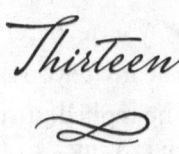

Annie was zippering her suitcase the next morning when there was a knock on her bedroom door. She jumped because up until then she had thought she was alone in the house. Molly and her mother had left at dawn to go to the café, and Val had told her last night that she would stop by after her morning walks.

It was only nine o'clock, meaning that unless one of her sisters had a change of plans, someone else had let themselves into the house.

"Annie?"

Annie froze at the sound of the familiar voice, and with a pounding heart, she opened the door of her bedroom.

"Dad?" He stood in the hallway, waiting to be allowed entrance, just like he had done a hundred times since she was old enough to start keeping her bedroom door closed around her teenage years. He never barged in on her the way her sisters did, but always stood back, letting her take the lead.

He wore one of his favorite blue plaid shirts tucked into

jeans, a look that usually brought Annie comfort, but even though she'd been back in town for only a week, and even though he'd lived in this house all her life, it felt strange to see him here all the same.

"Does Mom know you're here?" she asked, and then, more hopefully, "Did she invite you over?"

"I still have a key," he replied, surprising her. "It's still my home. Or at least, it still feels like my home."

Annie saw then the toll this separation had taken on him, and she opened the door wider, but he gave her a small smile and said, "I thought we could go talk on the porch. Like old times."

Like old times. The good old times. All those evenings after dinner, when the fireflies sparkled in the dark, and the only sound that could be heard was the chirping of crickets, and they'd talk about their days, or not talk at all, but just enjoy the sounds of nature. All those mornings when Annie's mom was already at the café, and the sky was a swirl of pink and purple, the smell of coffee rousing her from her warm bed, eventually something that they shared on the old swing, just the two of them, because her sisters were late sleepers.

"I'd like that," she said, feeling her throat lock up.

They slipped down the stairs like two fugitives even though the house was empty and would be for hours, and went out onto the porch. Her father took his usual side of the old swing, and she slid beside him. It creaked under their weight, the only noise other than the call of the birds.

"You left early last night," her father finally said.

Annie let out a long breath. She knew that they would

have to talk about it before she left. His retirement. Sean. The new era at the paper. Today wasn't just an ordinary Sunday. It was her father's first official day of retirement, and the paper's first official day under new leadership.

It was no longer a family legacy.

And that broke her heart.

And maybe she had no right to feel that way.

"I had to finish my article," she lied, knowing that it wasn't the first untruth she'd told him in recent years, but like the other, it was to protect him.

To see the shine of pride in his kind eyes.

He nodded along as if he believed her. And maybe he did. About both.

"I didn't get a chance to say thank you. That was some party, Annie, and it was even more special because you were there." His eyes were moist as he looked at her. "We've always had a special bond, you and me."

His hand found hers and held it tight.

Annie struggled to find her voice. "We do, Dad. We always will." And this was why she sensed that he had come to tell her something, not just to send her back to Seattle.

"Dad," she said carefully, knowing that he didn't want to open up, that he was a private man, humble, and that he wasn't one to complain. "Are you going to be okay?"

"Oh, honey." He sighed heavily. "I should be asking you that."

"Me?" She blinked at him. She'd thought she'd done a fine job convincing him that she was loving her life and job in Seattle and looking forward to a promotion that he would be partially responsible for her earning.

He stared at her for a moment and then shook his head. "What can I say? You'll always be my little girl. Even though you've gone on to do bigger things than I ever did—"

"No, Dad." Annie felt her breath catch, and she didn't think she could continue to lie, not even to protect him. "Success isn't about the size of your paycheck or how many people know your name. It's about how you feel at the end of the day."

And she felt empty. She had for too long.

"You're all grown up," he said, giving her hand another squeeze. "And to tell you the truth, I felt pretty bad at the end of the day yesterday."

"Because you're retiring?" She sat up a little straighter.

"Because I saw the look on your face when I announced my predecessor."

Oh. So he'd seen. She'd thought she'd done a good job of composing herself, slipping away to the bathroom to brush away the tears, and then out the back door.

"It was a...shock," she admitted, looking down at her lap as the memory of last night came back in full force. Sean standing beside her, trying to tell her something, her father standing before the room, and the look on Sean's face when the news was announced.

Sean had known, and he hadn't told her. He'd told her that she could trust him, but she shouldn't have.

"I understand why you did it," she said, struggling to meet her father's eyes. "Sean always loved the paper, and it's obvious that he still does."

"But you love it more," her father said. "The door was

always open for you, but I never invited you back in, and I should have."

"No, Dad," she said, refusing to let him take the blame. "I was the one who couldn't stop telling you about my great job in Seattle. And it is a great job. It's just...not for me."

"Then why did you stay?" He shifted in his seat to face her.

Annie sighed, feeling foolish now, knowing that she could have told her father anything, that he would have understood, because he loved her and only ever wanted the best for her.

But she only ever wanted the best for him, too.

And somewhere along the way, she'd thought that she was doing just that by sticking with something that took her away from the one thing she loved most. Including from him.

"I didn't want to let you down," she told him.

"Oh, Annie." Her father closed his eyes and shook his head. "The only way you could ever let me down is if you weren't true to yourself."

"But you kept saying how proud you were—"

"I was also proud when you won the second-grade coloring contest at the grocery store."

They shared a smile, and Annie wiped away a tear.

"I'm proud of everything you do, honey," he said softly. "So long as it makes you happy. And I encouraged you to take the job in Seattle because I saw that you weren't happy here."

"I wasn't then," Annie agreed. "But...I wasn't happy in Seattle. I'm still not."

Her father's face folded and it pained Annie to see it, only she understood now that it wasn't disappointment but empathy.

"Why didn't you ever tell me?" he pressed.

"I just...didn't want to let you down," Annie said with a shrug.

Her father's eyes misted. "I feel like I'm the one who let you down. I always thought we could tell each other anything."

"You were so proud and..." Annie sighed. "I didn't want you to think that everything you'd taught me was for nothing."

Except that now, in light of last night, that's exactly how it felt.

"I guess I saw what I wanted to see," her father said with a heavy sigh.

"I *let* you see what you wanted to see," she said, squeezing his hand now. "No one is at fault here, Dad."

"Oh, how I wish that were true." His smile was sad, but his eyes were warm when they met hers. "You and I are guilty of the same thing, aren't we? We both thought we were doing what was best for each other, even if we ended up hurting ourselves. The truth is that I never wanted to let you go, Annie. I missed you every single day, and all I ever really hoped was that someday you'd decide to come home."

"But you never asked me to," Annie said, her voice rising.

"I couldn't ask you to give up your happiness for mine," he replied simply.

Even if that's exactly what she'd done.

Mitch looked out on to the yard for a moment. "You know, I still haven't told you why I chose to retire."

No, he hadn't, and she hadn't pushed. She sensed that he would tell her if he wanted to, and she also knew that it couldn't have been an easy decision.

"That paper is your legacy, Dad. Are you ready to hand it off, no longer keep it in the family?"

She knew it was probably too late, but she had to try. She wouldn't give up on this family, and she sensed by the look in her father's eyes that he hadn't, either.

"Oh, Annie," he said, his voice thick with emotion. "Don't you see? That paper isn't my legacy. You are."

Annie took in that information, and let it sit.

"You and your sisters—and your mother—matter more than anything else ever could. I'm just sorry if I didn't make that clearer sooner."

"Are you leaving town, Dad?" Her heart was in her throat as she waited for the answer.

He looked at her sharply, then laughed. "No, never. I was born and raised here. My parents and grandparents were too! I could never leave Harmony Cove. But I do need to get out of that building."

"The *Herald*?" Annie stared at her father in disbelief. "But it was always your second home."

"Not always." His jaw set. "And now it's become my only home. And it's only made me all the more homesick, all the more aware of what I've lost. What I let pass me by."

"You mean Mom," she said gently.

Her father nodded. "She was right, you know, to give me the boot." He held up a hand before Annie could protest. "I let my work define my life when everything that really mattered was right here in these four walls. I never stopped to take your mother on a real vacation, and living on the Cape isn't a good enough excuse. I thought what I was doing was important—"

"It was," Annie told him, refusing to let him put himself down.

"But this family is more important," he said firmly. "That newspaper might be the voice of the town, and it's a title I held proudly, and with honor, but the real heart of this town, that's your mother. That's Sweet Harmony."

Annie thought of her article, her heart beating faster as she listened to her father's words. He's always had such a way with them.

"That photo you found of me working at the café reminded me of the early days when your mother and I were a team, back when I was writing the best stories, because I was sitting with the people, in the place they all loved most. A place your mother created and nurtured and grew. Oh, she didn't carry it over from the previous generations, but that's almost what makes it even more special. She made it for herself. For all of us. You, me, your sisters. Friends and neighbors."

Annie knew that it was all true. That maybe she'd taken it for granted. Just like her father had done. That all this time she'd thought he was the one who quietly handed the community what they needed every day, but maybe it wasn't just him, but her mother, too.

"You two are quite the pair," she remarked.

Or rather, were, she thought sadly to herself.

"I couldn't have done it without her," he said, his voice a little shaky. "And I've had to, all these months. And I don't want to anymore."

Annie understood now. He'd given it his all, but now it was the time to give to himself. And the woman he loved even more than this town.

She knew not to dig, but her reporter instinct told her that her father intended to try to win her mother back, and she could only hope that with a little time and love, they'd find their way back together.

Because sometimes, you had to stop searching for something better and enjoy what had been there all along and always would be.

Annie's father stood and hugged her after their conversation, but before he left, he handed her the morning's paper.

"The last one of an era," she said, almost afraid to touch it.

"Sean's story is on the front page," her father said gently.

Annie swallowed hard and nodded. She'd known it would be. All the more reason that she couldn't bring herself to lift her hands and accept it.

"I think you should read it," her father urged.

Annie had always been eager to please her dad, but today, just this once, she had to push back.

"Maybe one day," she managed.

"If you're mad at him for not telling you, then you should blame me," Mitch said. "I told him to keep the promotion to himself. Even from you. I wanted to be the one to share the news. I just didn't think to tell you first. I thought if I did..."

"That I'd stay." That was all she ever wanted to do.

"Please read the article," her father said, pushing the paper toward her.

Annie stepped back and shook her head. "I think that I've heard all Sean has to say, Dad. It's time that I accept that our lives went their separate ways a long time ago. He didn't choose me. He had his reasons, but he still didn't choose me."

Even now, he had chosen to stay in Harmony Cove for something other than her.

Her father opened his mouth and then closed it, nodding quietly. "I'll leave this here for you in case you change your mind." He set the paper on the porch swing and bent down and kissed her on the forehead, just like he did when she was a little girl. She buried her face in the soft cotton of his shirt, and she knew that even though today was different and strange and new for their family, it would all be okay somehow.

She waved him off from the porch, watching as he disappeared around the side of the house, hoping that one day soon, very soon, he'd be walking back up to it again.

This was his home. It was all of their home. And that was one thing that would never change.

Sean found his mother at the harbor, at her favorite bench with the best view of the boats coming in and out of Cape Cod Bay. She didn't look up when he took a seat beside her, but he saw her smile.

"It's beautiful, isn't it?" she remarked.

Sean wasn't sure if she meant the sleek sailboat that was gliding effortlessly across the water or the bright and sunny day, or just life in general. Right now, it was hard for him to appreciate any of the three, but he nodded all the same.

If his mother's illness had taught him anything, it was to make the most of every moment. And to hold on to those who you loved.

"Mom," he started to say and then stopped. He had planned to tell her the news himself, but the newspaper was folded in her lap, one hand protectively covering the front-page story. His story. The one he'd written about Mitch. For Mitch.

For the paper. For the town. For his home.

"I'm proud of you, Sean," his mother said, turning to him with shiny eyes.

Sean felt all the strength he'd built up these past few months, heck these past few years, start to break down, and he reached out to grab her hand and hold it as tight as he could, never wanting to let go.

"Not just of the story," she said pointedly.

"I'm not sure that Dad will feel the same way," Sean grumbled, looking back out on to the water. The sailboat was moving at a steady clip. Before long, it would be out of sight, disappearing into the horizon.

He glanced at his mother, and then back at the water,

swallowing hard.

"Oh, I wouldn't worry too much about that," his mother said with a sigh. "But I do worry about your father, and you should, too."

Sean frowned deeply, not following. "What do you mean I should worry about Dad? The man's always been fine at taking care of himself."

His mother raised an eyebrow. "That's what he'll have you believe. He puts on a brave face and a big show, but... he's scared. He always was, in a way. Of failure. But now, well, it's different."

Sean digested this information. He'd never understood his parents, how his mother's quiet and nurturing nature was so different from his father's brash energy. But now he understood that she saw a different side of the man. One that his father had never let him see.

"Your father may not know it yet, but he's going to need you, Sean," his mother said. "He'll...be grateful that you're staying in Harmony Cove."

"Mom." Sean heard his voice break.

His mother squeezed his hand and gave him one of her sweet smiles. "I know that the two of you always had a strained relationship. But...I have a feeling that things are going to change for the better for the two of you. That maybe...one good thing can come from this."

"Mom—"

She shook her head, smiling broader, but her eyes shone with tears. "He might appear to be strong, boorish even, but he's not as tough as he looks, Sean. He's scared. And when people are scared, sometimes they lash out. Be patient. I know it's not easy, and I know I'm asking a lot, but I've always been able to count on you."

And he'd always been able to trust her, even now.

"You have the opportunity for a fresh start, Sean," she said with a smile so full of hope that he felt like his heart could physically break. "Not many people get that in life."

Including her. Sean knew this was what she meant, and he also knew what she was asking of him. To make the most of it.

"You know what Dad wants me to do with my life," he told his mother.

"I know that your father sees so much potential in you," she surprised him by saying. "And he's always been worried that you wouldn't make the most of it. But that's for you to decide and for him to figure out, and accept."

Sean wished that he could have his mother's confidence, but for now, he'd have to have her faith.

"Maybe your father isn't the only person you can have a second chance with." She tipped her head. "I know you've been spending quite a bit of time with Annie."

Sean closed his eyes, his chest sinking heavily. "I think it's fair to say that it's over with Annie. That I've ruined things. Again."

His mother just patted his hand and smiled reassuringly. "Never say never, Sean. Never, ever, say never. So long as there is life, there is hope."

Sean gripped his mother's hand tighter, and they both turned their attention back to the water, watching the boats push out of the harbor, out to sea, onto their journey, to the great beyond.

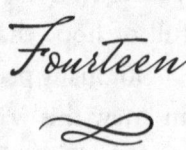

Fourteen

Sundays at the Sweet Harmony Café were always busy, and today was no exception. Annie was prepared to wait for a table if she had to, but when she stepped inside the brightly lit room that smelled of her mother's freshly baked rosemary bread, Molly caught her eye and motioned to an empty table near the window.

"How'd you manage to save it?" Annie whispered as she slid into a chair. She could see a line of tourists and locals waiting near the door, shooting her narrowed looks.

Molly set down a mug of coffee and said, "Dad called and told me you were on your way."

"Did he say anything else to you?" Annie asked carefully.

"Just that he loved the party," Molly said before a flicker of alarm passed over her soft features. "Why? Is there more I should know?"

Annie hesitated and then shook her head. If there was good news to share, she wanted her sister to hear it straight from the source.

"I also saved you the last blueberry muffin," Molly said with a wink. "I'll be right back with it."

One of the perks of being family.

One of the many, Annie thought with a smile as she watched her sister slip behind the counter, where her mother was boxing up baked goods for a customer. Her face was free of makeup today but somehow she'd never looked more beautiful, and under the worn apron was a simple long-sleeve white T-shirt.

Annie looked around the room, buzzing with conversation and laughter, the tables filled with plates of colorful and delicious-looking food, and she could only smile.

Maybe more than one thing.

With a happy sigh, she reached into her bag for her laptop to put the finishing touches on her email to her editor in Seattle, her fingers pausing when they brushed the newspaper her father had given her. The final edition.

She looked around the room, at the familiar faces sipping coffee and turning the pages of the Sunday *Herald*, catching up on all the community news, no doubt getting the full rundown of last night's party in Marcy's column.

The paper had lived to see a new day. Even though her father was no longer running it.

Not quite ready to face the final edition, she powered up her laptop and began quickly typing, never surer of her words than she was right now.

"I haven't seen you this fired up since our senior year," a voice said, and Annie's hands froze over the keyboard.

She looked up at Sean, who hovered next to her table, his

hands tucked into the pockets of his khakis, his hair tousled, his eyes a little tired.

"Something interesting?" he asked lightly.

As if this were so easy for him, swooping back into town, taking over not just her office but now her family's paper.

Her father's words came back to her, reminding her that maybe she wasn't being entirely fair, but nothing about love was fair, was it? She had loved this man; maybe a part of her always would.

And as recently as last night, she'd dared to believe that he still loved her, too.

"Very interesting," she replied, giving nothing else away.

They stared each other down for a moment, and then Sean gestured to the chair. "May I?"

Annie bristled, but then nodded, if only because she didn't want to make a scene. She'd have to find a way to coexist with this man and look past her hurt. To forget how much he'd let her down.

And how much he still meant to her.

"Putting the finishing touches on your article?" Sean asked. When she didn't reply, he said, "I take it you haven't read mine yet."

"No." It was a simple word, but saying it made her heart pound all the same. She knew that it would capture everything it needed to because he was a darn good reporter. And she knew that he would have done the story justice because he cared about the paper as much as she did.

And because he cared about her father.

Of these two things she was sure.

She just couldn't be sure that he cared the same way about her.

"I could get you a copy," he suggested.

"I have one in my bag, thanks," she said, barely sparing him a glance because it hurt too much to look at him and because her stomach still insisted on going all funny every time she did.

What was done was done. She understood why he hadn't told her just like she understood why her father had made the decision he did.

Just like she understood why Sean had left, all those years ago.

And why she had a few years later.

But understanding didn't stop the hurt. Or the consequences.

"I'm not mad at you because you're the new editor of the paper," she said with a heavy sigh.

His brow knitted. "You're not?"

She hesitated. "I always thought when my father retired that I would take over, but I've been in Seattle, and I've been up for a big promotion, and..." And she'd blown her chance at the job she'd really wanted all this time.

"My father thinks highly of you," she said firmly, to herself as much as to him, knowing that it was true. "As a reporter and...as a person."

Sean raised his eyebrows in surprise. "I learned from the best."

Annie swallowed the lump in her throat. She knew that he wasn't referring to any of their college professors.

"You're a fine reporter yourself, Annie Baker," Sean said

with a sad smile. "I have no doubt that you're going to get that big promotion if that's what you want."

If that's what she wanted. But it wasn't. It never was. It was only ever what she'd led everyone to believe.

Including, she realized, the man sitting across the table from her right now. The man who had taken the highest position at her family's paper, thinking that she didn't want it.

"You can read my article first," she said, swinging her laptop toward him, knowing that the time had come for him to read her words, and maybe for her to give him the same courtesy.

Decisions had been made, consequences had happened, but maybe, just maybe, all was not lost.

She glanced over at her mother, who grinned at her from behind the counter, and her heart swelled with hope.

Sean leaned across the table and scanned the screen of her laptop, his expression showing his surprise before he narrowed his eyes and looked back up at her.

"I'm leaving my position," she clarified just in case the resignation letter didn't make that obvious. "I'm not going back to Seattle. I'm going to stay right here, in Harmony Cove."

"I had a feeling you'd say that," he said, grinning slowly. "Not because of me, but because I think that like me, you never really wanted to leave in the first place."

She nodded quietly. "Sometimes you have to leave behind the things you love most to understand just how much you miss them."

"And I've missed you," he said, his voice husky.

Annie could feel the eyes on her, and not because she'd gotten a priority table. They were looking at them, Sean and Annie. The golden couple.

Or so they'd once been.

"I think it's my turn to show you my article," he replied, slapping a copy of the Sunday paper down on the table, always the thickest of the week.

Annie huffed out a sigh. A deal was a deal, and she knew that she'd eventually be curious enough to read it, once the hurt faded and her heart stopped feeling like someone had reached in and ripped it out.

She slid the paper across the table and unfolded it. Sure enough, Sean's article took up the entire front page, along with several photos of her father over the years. She had to hand it to Sean; he'd chosen good ones. There was one of him and Marcy, when they were both younger, standing beside their father, her grandfather. And another of Mitch, sitting at his desk, his wire-rimmed glasses perched on the end of his nose, looking up at the camera, a hint of a smile on his mouth. And the last one was of her father, another candid, standing with a group of townspeople, some she could name, and others whose names she'd forgotten over the years, his arms over their shoulders, his smile wide.

"The voice of the people," she said as she absorbed the title, feeling the lump rise in her throat, darn it. She read each word, so beautifully crafted, as she knew it would be, and even if she'd wanted to skim it, she had to stop and take in every word, because this article wasn't about Sean or her or their messy history. It was about her father. His legacy. And her family.

She read about Mitch's integrity, his gentle way and humble nature, even when he was the rightful owner, who could have done as he pleased, how he saw journalism as a calling, how he strived to do right by the people whose stories he told.

How he loved his family.

And how he had announced his retirement when the entire town was gathered, together.

It was here, at the bottom of the article, that Annie felt she couldn't continue. She started to push the paper away, but Sean stopped her.

"Please read it through to the end." His gaze met hers, soft and dark, and pleading.

Annie pinched her mouth, reminding herself that for her father, for the paper, she would see this through to the final word, because this article honored him, and Sean did it justice.

The article went on to say that Mitch was retiring, that he hoped to travel and spend more time with his family, and that—

She frowned, but her entire body was shaking by the time she looked back up at Sean, who was smiling now.

"It says..." She looked back down again, to be sure that she hadn't read it wrong. Maybe it was a misprint. Maybe there would be a retraction. Or maybe...

"'The paper will henceforth be run by coeditors-in-chief Sean Morrison and Annie Baker, who will carry down the Baker family legacy,'" Sean finished for her.

Yes, that was exactly what it said. But that was not what

her father had told her. Not last night. And not this morning.

Annie stared at Sean, who was grinning broadly. Her heart was pounding so hard that she wasn't sure she could speak, or what she could even say. Her mind whirred with thoughts of last night, and her conversation with her father this morning, and how any of this had come to be.

"But my dad was putting the article to bed last night before the party," she said, trying to make sense of this, knowing that he'd made that clear before he turned off the lights for the final time. "It was already going to print."

"Good thing we got the change in just in time," Sean said simply.

"But—"

"But nothing," Sean said. "I'm not going to stand in the way of you taking over your family's business. And...I'm hoping that nothing can stand in the way of us."

Annie felt the tears threatening to spill, and for once she didn't care if Marcy might be peering through the windows. For the first time in years, she was crying out of happiness, and she wanted the entire town, and all the people in it who she loved, to share it with her.

"I talked to your father after the party. I knew the moment I saw the look on your face that this was what you wanted. All you ever wanted. I couldn't take that from you, and I never would have wanted to," he said. "So we changed the article. We got it out right before it went to print. Guess it was meant to be." He grinned.

Annie, however, could only stare as she played out this

turn of events. Her father—and Sean—hurrying to make things right. Not just for her. But for them.

For us, she thought, staring at Sean. "You're wrong about one thing," she said. "This isn't all I ever wanted."

He frowned at her, but this time, she couldn't help being the one to smile.

"This. You. Me. And the paper. And this town. That's all I ever wanted. To share it with you."

His hand reached out and found hers, but rather than hold it tight, he stood, pulling her up with him. The entire café seemed to go quiet as he took a step around the table and reached his arms down to her waist.

She looked up into the face of the man she'd tried so hard to forget and now wouldn't have to, but instead of rising up to meet his kiss, she waited, letting this moment sink in, committing it to her heart, because this was one that she knew she would always want to remember.

Epilogue

The last edition of the paper as Annie had always known it to be ran on Sunday, but the first edition of the paper as Annie had always dreamed it could be ran on Monday, after a long day at the office, too many cups of coffee, and a few, according to the Harmony Happenings column, romantic distractions.

The boxes landed with a thud at five o'clock that morning, and Annie and Sean weren't the only ones to greet the delivery man. Her father stood there, too, admittedly in his bathrobe this time instead of a proper shirt and slacks, and when he pulled the first newspaper from the stack, he looked at her with more pride than he had in all the visits she'd made over the years, talking up her job in Seattle.

Annie stood back, watching as he read the front-page headline, wondering if she'd been right to run her story—her article, the one she'd finished after her talk with her dad yesterday. Sean had given her his blessing, and after moving back into her office, she'd worked tirelessly on it for the remainder of the day.

"What do you think, Dad?" she asked with bated breath, knowing that, like her, he was a fast reader, even if today he did seem to be taking his time with each word.

"I think," he said as he tucked the paper under his arm and removed his reading glasses, "that I have never been more proud."

Annie folded herself into his warm arms and let him plant a kiss on her forehead, before stepping back to take Sean's arm.

"We did it," she said, looking up at him, still struggling to believe that it was real, that after years of hardship, and a week of uncertainty, just when life felt like it was at its worst, it somehow never felt better.

"All we have to do now is deliver these," Sean said with a glance at his watch. The kids who ran their routes would be arriving soon.

"If you don't mind, I'd like to deliver this one to the house," Annie's father said, tapping the paper under his arm. "Unless you want to be there when your mother sees your first edition."

"These words don't just come from me," Annie reassured her father. "They represent what I think everyone in town believes."

"Certainly what I do." Mitch pulled in a breath. "And with that, I think it's time for me to start the first day of the rest of my life and let you two get on with yours."

"Dad—" Annie couldn't help but stop him before he turned away. "Are you sure? That this is what you want?"

"I won't say no to being a contributor every once in a while," he said with a warm smile. "But yes, Annie. I've never been more sure."

She nodded. Neither, she thought, had she.

Sean squeezed her hand until her father was out of sight, not shuffling up the stairs of the office building to the lonely apartment, but this time, heading in a different direction.

Today, like herself and Sean, Mitch Baker was going to end the day where he was meant to be.

"I don't think your mother is expecting this," Sean said.

Annie knew that he wasn't talking about her father giving a tap on the windowpane, or perhaps just opening the door, after so many long and quiet months.

She pulled another paper off the stack and looked at the front page.

Like her father, her mother quietly did her work with love and thought, not asking for reward or acknowledgment, and certainly not the attention that she so deserved.

"We did them proud," she told Sean, knowing that it meant every bit as much to him as to her.

"We did ourselves proud," Sean said, grinning until his eyes crinkled.

A picture of her parents, young and in love, sitting at a table, stared back at her. It was, true to her style, a community piece, featuring one of Harmony Cove's brightest treasures, the Sweet Harmony Café. It wasn't just the best spot for a cup of chowder or a warm haven for a mug of cocoa. The rotating menu was thoughtfully prepared with produce fresh from Sharon Baker's garden, which was planted with love and tended with care, much like the town itself. The café was home to young courtships, lifelong friendships, and even true love.

It was full of good food, family, friends, laughter, and, above all, heart.

It was, quite simply, home.

About the Author

Olivia Miles is a two-time *USA Today* bestselling author of heartwarming women's fiction and small town romance. After growing up in New England, she now lives on the shore of Lake Michigan with her family and an adorable pair of dogs.

Visit www.OliviaMilesBooks.com for more.

www.ingramcontent.com/pod-product-compliance
Lightning Source LLC
LaVergne TN
LVHW030319070526
838199LV00069B/6507